KRIS LONGKNIFE'S REPLACEMENT

ADMIRAL SANTIAGO ON ALWA STATION

MIKE SHEPHERD

KL & MM BOOKS

Published by KL & MM Books
December 2016
Copyright © 2016 by Mike Moscoe

This book is a work of fiction set 400 years in humanity's future. Any similarity between present people, places, or events would be spectacularly unlikely and is purely coincidental.

This book is written and published by the author. Please don't pirate it. I'm self-employed. The money I earn from these sales allow me to produce more stories to entertain you. I'd hate to have to get a day job again. If this book comes into your hands free, please consider going to your favorite e-book provider and investing in a copy so I can continue to earn a living at this wonderful art.

I would like to thank my wonderful cover artist, Scott Grimando, who did all my Ace covers and will continue doing my own book covers. I also am grateful for the editing skill of Lisa Müller, Edie Lemonier, and, as ever, Ellen Moscoe.

Rev 1.0

Note to long time readers of Kris's saga: Due to the limitations that impact self-published books, the small caps that has highlighted talk on Nelly Net has been replaced ALL CAPS BUT IN A SMALLER FONT.

eBook ISBN-13: 978-1-64211-0036
Print ISBN-13: 978-1-64211-0029

Kris Longknife: Bold

Vicky Peterwald: Target

Vicky Peterwald: Survivor

Vicky Peterwald: Rebel

Mike Shepherd writing as Mike Moscoe in the Jump Point Universe

First Casualty

The Price of Peace

They Also Serve

Rita Longknife: To Do or Die

Short Specials

Kris Longknife: Training Daze

Kris Longknife : Welcome Home, Go Away

Kris Longknife's Bloodhound

Kris Longknife's Assassin

The Lost Millennium Trilogy Published by KL & MM Books

Lost Dawns: Prequel

First Dawn

Second Fire

Lost Days

Kris Longknife's Replacement
By
Mike Shepherd

Grand Admiral Sandy Santiago is a woman with a very big problem.

How does a mere mortal fill the shoes of one of those damn Longknifes? Worse, the shoes she has to fill are Kris Longknife's. She's got birds, cats, and the occasional murderous alien.

How does a girl get this lucky?

1

rand Admiral Sandy Santiago paused at the top of the gangplank of the USS *Wasp* to take a deep breath. It came in tasting of the usual mixtures she'd come to expect on a space station: machine oil, plastics, and human sweat with undertones of other, less savory scents we humans give the air. This breath, however, was loaded with a whole lot more. Sandy had come face to face with just how big a challenge she faced.

She was taking over a command from Admiral, Her Royal Highness, Kris Longknife. Of course, there was also the added spice to her life of very likely getting killed. As a Santiago, she well knew how many of her family had bled and died for the Longknife legend.

Still, a command on the far side of the galaxy had to be about as independent as an admiral could ask for. That challenge had grabbed her and propelled her all the way out here.

And now that she'd gotten her first briefing from Kris Longknife herself, she felt a little bit poleaxed.

I didn't see any of that coming.

Sandy rendered proper honors and crossed the brow. As she strode along, she began organizing all that had been thrown at her: an admiral pregnant, suicide missions fought off, every single one of them. Five - no six - huge alien mother ships fought and destroyed in three different battles, the last one involving thousands of ships on their side against all that we humans had managed to scrape up, a little over two hundred. Oh, and 160 of that huge human battle fleet had burned their reaction tanks dry and were drifting in orbit hundreds of light years from their base in desperate need of a refueling mission.

Kris had a busy couple of months. Fortunately, Sandy was well past that baby thing and looking forward to spoiling grandkids and returning them to her sons and daughters when they became troublesome. She chuckled to herself. She'd started longevity at thirty. While she could still do PT with the Marines on the USS *Victory*, there was no way this admiral was going to get pregnant.

No way, no how.

Which still left a whole lot on Sandy's plate.

She was so lost in her thoughts about all she needed to do that she hardly noticed when a three-star admiral, tall, chiseled and graying, along with a petite, young, female civilian that looked ready to explode, crossed her path.

When their presence impinged on Sandy's notice, she fixed them with a jaundiced eye and cleared her throat.

The two of them eyed one another, then, evidently experienced with each other enough to read the other's mind, the young woman said, "You go first, Admiral Benson."

"Benson?" Sandy echoed, "I thought the king sent you out here for a civilian post. Dockyards or something."

"Out on Alwa Station, Admiral, we repair them, we build more, and then, when the time comes, we fight them as well.

I commanded the Reserve Fleet under the admiral, here," he said with a nod toward the *Wasp* where said admiral was busy gestating – and recovering from one hell of a battle.

"Reserve Fleet?" Sandy said, frowning as her mind raced through the skimpy debriefing she'd just gotten from Kris Longknife. "Didn't you just hold the last jump into Alwa against the final push by the bug-eyed monsters?"

The man's face lit up with pure, one hundred percent pride. "That we did, ma'am. Me, and most of my yard birds along with any of Pipra's factory workers willing to volunteer, or Granny Rita's Colonials or the odd and sod Rooster or Ostrich that we could train up to stand a watch. We may have been a very mixed bag and nowhere near Navy squared away, but we fought the damn bug-eyed monsters and we got 'em good."

"Well done, Admiral. Now, would you mind following me back to my flag? I think there's some odds and ends that need tidying up."

"That's what we need to talk about, ma'am. Those odds, and the next set of ins. Grand Admiral, may I present Pipra Strongarm, Kris's right arm gal running the industrial side of the show out here. She oversees the independent operators out in the asteroids that mine the stuff that's shipped down to the moon fabricators that Pipra also bosses. A lot of the stuff that comes out of them gets shipped up here. Then me and my yard birds use it to patch together ships that the Navy dings, dents, and busts up. With what's left over, we spin together brand spanking new ships. You wouldn't believe what comes out of my yard and the three or four other dockyards that nice folks back home have been kind enough to ship out here. Besides me and defense gobbling stuff up, her fabs also make the goodies that the Colonials like and the Alwans demand."

Sandy nodded at the young woman, not sure how this all fit together . . . or mattered to her. "Fine, I'd be glad to talk to both of you later, but I've got the wreckage of a battle to police up. I understand from Kris that she's got much of a Battle Fleet out there to hell and gone running on fumes, and I need to get some reaction mass out to them soonest," Sandy said, quick marching for her flag.

Both the Navy officer and the civilian quick-marched right along beside her. "Yes, Admiral, that's why we think you need to talk to both of us now, and maybe Granny Rita and the Colonial's First Minister Ada, too."

Sandy gave him a gimlet eye, but didn't quite give him the line that demanded, "If you're so smart, why ain't there more stripes on your coat than mine?"

"Begging your pardon, ma'am," Admiral Benson went on, if a bit uncomfortably, "it's likely not safe for you to send the ships you just brought in out there. Leastwise, you're more likely to lose more of yours than I'd lose of mine."

Now Sandy did give him the Look. "You want to explain yourself, admiral?"

And be fast about it, went unsaid.

"Are you aware of something called crystal armor that they've developed on Earth?"

"I'm aware of it. None of it has gotten out to the rim yet. Why?"

"Well, ma'am, a couple of squadrons of Earth battle-cruisers showed up out here a while back. Between the scientists and engineers we had on station, Pipra's industries and my yard hands, we kind of reverse engineered the stuff and managed to coat every ship in our fleet with it before this last dust up."

Sandy came to a halt. The look she now gave him was full on surprise. With maybe a bit of awe tossed in.

"*You* put that *weird* armor on your *entire* fleet?"

"Yes, Admiral," Benson said with a proud grin. "And there are a lot fewer dead sailors out there because we did, ma'am."

"And you got all of that stuff out of your moon fabricators?" she said, glancing at the civilian.

"You're damn right we did, ma'am. You ever try to tell a Longknife you couldn't give her what she wanted?"

"Not recently," Sandy muttered, then, remembering she needed to be on her flag bridge, kept walking, but slower, so the woman wouldn't have to run so much to keep up.

"Okay, Admiral Benson, tell me what you think I need to know about operations on Alwa Station."

"You got a week?"

She glared at him.

"He's not joking, ma'am," Pipra put in, defending the Navy man. "The way Kris Longknife has been running things, it doesn't fit any book, and frankly, if she hadn't, I don't think any of us would still be alive."

"Okay, give me the short form. You can give me the long one later."

Again, the two locals exchanged glances. This time, the young woman took over the conversation. "I'm assuming that you don't want to be running your ships around here without a coating of crystal armor."

"How long will it take you to glue or whatever you do with the crystal to get it wrapped around my ships? I brought in sixty-four of what Kris is calling battlecruisers."

The business woman rubbed her eyes, then looked off toward the distant end of the space station. When she started speaking, it was slowly. "That all depends on how fast we can get production up and running again. Ben, can you stand down some of my workers?"

"BatRon 13 is first on my decommissioning list," Admiral Benson answered. *"Furious, Enterprise, Audacious, Resolute, Proud Unicorn, Lucky Leprechaun, Kikukei* and *Temptress* are crewed pretty much by my dockyard workers with some of your people added on and a few Roosters and Ostriches tossed in for good measure. We'll get the most labor out of those ships. If I shake out the V class, *Valiant, Vanguard, Vindictive,* and *Victorious*, I should have enough to handle our damaged ships as well as up armor at least sixteen of your ships, Admiral."

"Assuming I can get the crystal growing again," Pipra growled.

"Assuming?" Sandy demanded.

"You know, Granny Rita's going to be screaming for farming equipment and the Alwans will be hooting for their trade goods."

Admiral Santiago was not following this conversation. Grand Admirals do not appreciate having to listen to conversations that meant nothing to them.

Grand admirals did not have to put up with this kind of noise, either.

"Explain yourselves," she demanded.

Again, the young woman took the lead. "My fabricators knock out what the admiral here needs for his yards, but they also have to meet the demands of the human Colonials and the Alwan birds. As you may have heard a moment ago, we've got Colonials and Alwans standing watch side by side with your sailors. I've got Colonials and Alwans doing shifts in my fabs. We're getting pretty mixed up and matched, but you got to feed the cow's front end before you can milk guns and butter out her back end. You following me?"

Sandy scowled. "The picture is disgusting, but you say Kris has been juggling all of this?"

"*We've* been juggling all this," Pipra said, forcefully. "Kris, us, them, all, and anyone handy. You following me?"

"I think so," Sandy admitted. "I was briefed that some factories and yards had been flown out here to provide some sort of support force. I didn't really expect, from the tone of voice of those who mentioned all this stuff, that you'd be running all of it at full bore."

"Full bore and balls to the wall," Admiral Benson said. "I'm not sure any of us thought we could do half of what we've done, but when you've got Kris Longknife giving you The Look, you don't tell her you can't, you tell her she'll have it ahead of schedule and under price."

"Even if we haven't figured out how to price anything in this crazy economy," Pipra added, making a face like she'd been made to swallow a lemon.

They had reached Sandy's flagship. The canvas stretched between the guardrails on either side of the brow was blue with the proud name *Victory* in bold white letters. Someone had added five stars in a circle as well.

"Please come aboard," Admiral Santiago said, leading the way. "I know we've only scratched the surface of the mess you're dropping in my lap. Remember, there are still those hungry ships out there, starving for reaction mass."

2

"If I may," Admiral Benson noted, settling into a seat across from Sandy at the conference table in her day quarters, "you face three problems."

Benson had waited to make his point while Sandy had coffee and sandwiches brought in. That also allowed time for Captain Van Velder, Sandy's chief of staff, and Mondi Ashigara, her operations chief, to join them.

"Only three problems?" Mondi asked. The tall, thin woman was a stickler for details.

"No doubt, these three will spawn their own crop with more heads to lop off," Pipra answered.

"Getting back to our three problems," Benson said, going forward. "The alien wolf packs have designed two new classes of ships. One is fast, though lightly armed and armored. Some of them may be wandering around our flanks or rear areas. The other class is the opposite: huge things we call door knockers. They have thick rock armor and a massive number of lasers ready to fire in all directions. They weren't included in the main battle Kris just fought. Those door knockers were seen to slip out one of the more distant jumps after we annihilated the main force. Admiral, it might behoove you to chase them down and destroy them before they report back to whatever wolf packs are still out there. We really don't want them all in the know of how we demolished these last four."

Mondi was taking furious notes, calling up reports on her reader and looked ready to come out of her chair. There was a lot to like about Mondi's eagerness. Still, Sandy knew when to keep her leash tight.

"And the other two?" Sandy said.

"We've got something like 160 ships, minus losses, out there at what we call System X that are sucking the last fumes from their reaction mass tanks. They've got to be refueled, and the damaged ones convoyed back here for some serious repair work in the yards. There are also three massive and heavily damaged beam ships that are likewise in desperate need of a return escort. The worst damaged one was last seen limping out of the system in any direction that didn't look to have any bug-eyed monsters. We used all three of them desperately hard. Likely we'll need to completely rebuild them before we dare fire one of them again. Even after we do that, the good Lord only knows what kind of work we can expect to get out of them."

"And lastly?" Sandy said, not happy about the length of this problem list, but not able to find fault with it, either.

"There's the matter of whether or not your new arrivals are up to fighting by Alwan standards, ma'am."

"We arrived ready for a fight," Van put in, storm clouds forming in his bushy eyebrows.

"No, doubt, Captain, but did you arrive ready to fight the Kris Longknife and Alwa Defense Sector's way? Begging the admiral's pardon, but did Phil Taussig get a chance to pass along to the home fleet how Kris fights her battlecruisers?"

"You mean jinksing all over the place?" Sandy replied. "He mentioned something about that. Admiral, I was there when Lieutenant Kris Longknife took her fast attack boats in to get those six battleships someone sent out to blast Wardhaven back into the stone age. She and those boats did some wild jigs. She's not trying to do something like that with a ship this big, is she?" Sandy said, glancing around at the bulkheads and overhead.

"A tiny slip of a mosquito boat was one thing. A sixty or seventy thousand ton, near-capital ship? Even a Longknife couldn't be that crazy."

The two locals exchanged glances.

Damn, she is that crazy.

Admiral Benson chose his words carefully, as you'd expect from a Navy officer who had thirty plus years of explaining the facts to ignorant elephants. "Begging the admiral's pardon, ma'am, but yes, the admiral won't have any ship, picket, or battlecruiser stay on any set course for more than two, maybe three seconds. That's how we fight, win, and stay alive on Alwa Station."

"You can't jump a ship this size around like a spit kit," Van said, as absolute as any Navy captain ever had been.

"You'll want to have your ships' computers talk to Kris's Nelly. It involves widening the piping between the reactor to the maneuvering jets, and doubling the number of those suckers, as well," Benson said. When faced with the look of rejection, he didn't wilt, but went on. "You'll also likely want to upgrade your high gee stations. On Alwa Station, they not only have to accommodate acceleration along a single axis, but also right, left, up, down, faster, slower, and maybe even a bit of torque. Kris Longknife is as rough on her crew as she is on her ships."

"You're serious," Van said, playing devil's advocate so his boss wouldn't have to.

"Dead serious," Benson answered. "That's why I was suggesting that if you do decide to send out a squadron or two on a refueling mission, that you also take along a squadron and a half of mine to escort you. That way, on the way to System X, they can help you drill in some of the bobbing and weaving we do out here. You don't want to be unprepared if you run into any stray monsters that didn't get The Word they lost."

"And I'm thinking of chasing myself some of those door knockers you mentioned," Sandy said.

"Again, ma'am, I know I suggested we see if we can chase them down, but you might want to be very careful before you follow them through a jump point."

Sandy raised an eyebrow. "Because?"

"We've been bushwhacking them as they come through the jumps."

"You can guard jumps?" Mondi said, incredulously.

"You may have noticed some ships keeping guard back a bit from the jump you just came through," Admiral Benson said.

"I thought that was some kind of space station," Mondi answered.

"Nope. You were looking at three ships docking together using a Smart Metal hookup to anchor them in one place. They rotate. They get some down for the crew's health and at least one of them is always in a position to shoot at anything that comes through that jump. We've been picking off suicide boats, fast little buggers. So far, we've been batting a thousand. We have to. We miss one and a whole lot of people and birds will die on the planet below."

"Can the aliens do something like that?" Mondi asked.

"I don't think they can, or have tried. Remember, we spin out a Smart Metal beam to anchor to. They'd need to carry some regular metal beam around with them. Still, getting back to those door knockers, Admiral. I wouldn't put it past those aliens to leave a couple dozen of those things standing guard over a jump to buy time for the rest to get away. It might be pretty putrid in those ships, but they would have enough power to shoot you full of holes if you jumped through without looking first."

"Looking first?" was again Mondi.

"We've got a periscope that lets us look through the jump. You have to kind of drift up to the jump, but you can see what's on the other side."

Sandy wiped at her eyes with the palms of both hands. "Is it always like this around Kris Longknife? Everything's different?"

"That's what I've found," Benson answered. "But I'm not complaining, ma'am. We're still alive. I don't think when they dispatched us here that anyone was laying any kind of odds that we would be alive and still fighting after this long."

"And winning," Pipra put in. "Don't forget the winning. I kind of like winning. It lets me keep breathing oxygen. I really like that habit."

Sandy nodded. She did like being alive.

"Okay, Van, I'm leaving you behind to work with Ben, here. Get our ships moving into his yards as soon as docks are available and get that new, fancy armor added to the ships."

"And you're going to have all the fun," Van grumbled.

"Yep. Mondi, prepare BatRon 1 and 2 to go to space. We'll use them as tankers while the local ships escort us and show us how it's done on Alwa Station."

"We, ma'am?" Van asked cautiously,

"We, Van. I'll be taking the task force out. I want to get a decent feel for what the situation is out here. I'm not going to get that feel sitting at a dock."

"Aye, aye, Admiral," Mondi said. "BatRon 1 and 2 to sortie in as soon as possible."

"In two hours," Sandy amended the order.

"Two hours?"

"And if a captain can't get his boat to answer all bells, get a replacement from one of the other squadrons. No doubt, you'll have plenty of volunteers. Admiral," Sandy said, turning to Benson. "Will your twelve ships be able to get up steam in two hours?"

"I suspect I'd better go tell them."

"Are we done here?" Sandy said, starting to rise.

"May I have a moment of your time?" Pipra said, staying solidly in her seat.

"Who are you, again?" Sandy said. She'd wondered why Benson had had a civilian shadow. She was not all that pleased with talking about Navy operations with someone not in uniform in the room.

Admiral Benson was halfway to the door, but he turned to put in, "As I mentioned before, ma'am, she's been Kris Longknife's right arm where production is concerned. She's been a life saver from my perspective. Instead of bitching and moaning about her profit margin, she's seen to it that we got what we needed when we needed it. She's good people, Admiral."

Sandy would decide that for herself.

"You've got one minute, talk," Sandy said.

"I need your help, Admiral."

Sandy's eyes grew wide. "My help?"

"Admiral, Kris Longknife made the point abundantly

clear that we all either pulled together or we'd all die in one big heap. I haven't always liked what she did to me and mine, but I had to respect her. As Admiral Benson said, we've all pulled together. My problem is that Alex Longknife has just dumped a whole new management team on top of me and they've already ripped me up one side and down the other for not showing a profit."

Sandy had thirty-seven years in this gal's Navy. Commanding ships and Sailors was her forte. Suffering contractors was something she did her best to avoid. Her first thought was to tell this woman thank you for the heads-up and send her on her way.

Sandy held her tongue and, instead, turned to Ben, now standing at the door.

"You need this industrial base?"

"Desperately, Admiral."

She turned back to the woman. "Why would Alex Longknife send a new management team out here?"

The woman actually looked embarrassed. "I was a junior vice president when I arrived here. There was a CEO and a senior vice president who were supposed to run the show. Instead, once Kris Longknife pointed out the hazards of our position and her demand that the Navy be the center of our efforts, those two wandered off and drank themselves to death. Since I was with the Longknife group, and I had Kris Longknife's attention, I ended up running the whole shebang."

Pipra paused to take a deep breath. "However, the truth was, I was the Junior Vice President for Human Resources, ma'am. I was supposed to hold coats, not take over and run things. I suspect when Commodore Taussig went back to Wardhaven, my status may have come up in some fashion. Anyway, Alex sent an entire new team out here."

Again, the woman paused. "I also think they saw a chance to make a killing, even if it drove a plant on Alwa to extinction and strained our relationships with the locals. Are you aware of the unique plant we shipped back and its very unusual aspects?"

"Do you mean am I aware that there's a plant out here that might revolutionize microminiatures, if not nano activity, by jacking up their power by several orders of magnitude? Yes, I know of the thing."

"Alex thinks that in three, maybe five years, his labs will develop artificial versions of the plant's mitochondria. Right now, though, they can make a killing in the market by bringing bushels of the plant back to human space and selling an ounce of it for a million bucks or more. They're ready to send teams down into the Ostrich section of the planet below and scour up every leaf they can find."

The woman fell silent, leaving it to Sandy to grasp the full impact of her boss's plans.

Sandy turned to Admiral Benson who still hadn't made it out the door. He was just finishing up saying something into his comlink, though. "Ben, how would this impact our relations with the whatever-they-are? Sometimes you call them Roosters, other times Ostriches. Which are they?"

Admiral Benson cleared his throat. "The Roosters and Ostriches are about as different as say Old Earth's Europeans, Africans and Asians. The thing you need to know is that the Ostriches are fighters and very territorial. Kris Longknife had to walk pretty careful around those Ostriches' feet, and even she was shot at once. While she got some land grants from the Ostriches, she was careful to leave them the rivers and large streams. If someone starts mucking around without permission, they could get their head kicked off their shoulders. And I mean literally, not figuratively. Those suckers can kick."

He glanced at Pipra. "Also, the Ostriches have been the most eager to get jobs up here at my yards, at Pipra's fabrication facilities and aboard our battlecruisers. If someone pisses them off, we could lose a whole lot of goodwill and good workers. May I make a recommendation, Admiral?"

"Please do. I don't much care for this bucket of snakes."

"Kris Longknife is still the senior officer of Nuu Enterprises in the Alwa System. If she's got anything like the temper my wife had during the last month or so of her pregnancies, I'd have Pipra trot over to the *Wasp* and see how Kris likes her grandpa's latest dump on her. My guess would be that the ship that's supposed to go back loaded with water plants might instead just be carrying a few damn fool business types."

"Why didn't you take it to her in the first place?" Sandy said, scowling at the industrialist.

The woman accepted the scowl, and quickly said her piece. "I was headed to see Kris when I ran into you coming off the *Wasp*, Admiral. Everyone knows that you've replaced her. It's not at all clear who's the boss of anything now."

Sandy found she had to agree with the woman. "I just found out how many hats that woman wears. Admiral commanding Alwa's defenses, Viceroy of the King on Alwa, CEO of Nuu Enterprises, and pretty much straw boss of all the industrial base operating here. Who in God's name dumped all that on one poor woman?"

"Ray Longknife, I believe," Benson provided dryly.

"There's a reason why we Santiagos hate Longknifes, and he's a huge part of it. Okay, Pipra, it's been great meeting you. Please get off my ship before we pull up the gangplank. Do have fun talking this over with Kris and feel free to darken my door anytime you need to. I suspect I'll be seeing a lot of you. Ben, just exactly what is your part in this crime scene? I hear you giving orders to a reserve fleet, but also running yards."

"I'm Commander, Base Forces for Kris, what little we've managed to patch together of a base force," the admiral said. "If it don't sail, it's mine. That is until all hell breaks loose. Then we down tools and jump on things that do move and go out to fight for our lives."

"Alwa Station," Sandy said, but didn't quite spit. "You do everything different."

"*We* do everything different, ma'am. You're one of *us* now, Grand Admiral," Benson said.

"And may God help *us* all. Now, I've got a fleet to get away from the pier."

"Good luck and Godspeed," Admiral Benson said, then quickly led the civilian from Sandy's day quarters.

"God help us all," Sandy whispered as they closed the door. "Ray Longknife, what have you gotten me into this time?"

Grand Admiral Sandy Santiago's flagship, *Victory*, led her ad hoc task force through the final jump into System X. Even at 45,000 kilometers per hour, her usually sleek ships waddled like ducks; each battlecruiser bulged with three times its normal reaction mass.

"Admiral," Comm reported, "the emergency frequencies are saturated."

Sandy was quickly behind Comm, looking over his shoulder. Hundreds of emergency beepers demanded their attention. Some showed yellow to orange on the board. Way too many glowed red. Many of the red were flashing. Whoever was in that survival pod did not have long to live unless rescue came real soon.

"Admiral Hart," she said, raising the admiral who had led his twelve battlecruisers through the jump first. Benson lent her Hart not only as an escort for her lumbering elephants but to also demonstrate on the way out, to their embarrassing edification, that big battlecruisers could jitterbug like nobody's business.

"Yes, Admiral."

"You are detached to render all assistance."

"We're already on our way. Three minutes ago, I ordered my ships to accelerate.

"We'll be at four gees in about two minutes," he answered

Sandy glanced at the regional scan on the main screen. His ships were already pulling away from hers.

Gladly, Sandy would have followed him, but a survey of the system showed a battle fleet in orbit around a burned-out husk of a planet orbiting a neutron star. "Comm, send to task fleet, 'Accelerate to two gees smoothly, set course for the neutron star'."

Acknowledgments came back quickly and the two squadron commanders did their job of getting their battle-cruisers into acceleration mode. This force would take a full fifteen minutes to put on just two gees.

While the fleet moved out, the sensor team on the *Victory* completed its assessment of the system. It was brutal.

It would be half a day before any communications arrived from Admiral Kitano and the survivors of her battle fleet. In the meantime, the visual and electromagnetic analysis of the system showed one hell of a battle had been fought here. The humans had won. The aliens had lost. That didn't mean that one hell of a butcher's bill hadn't been paid.

Scattered through the fields of survivor pods was fragmentary wreckage of destroyed ships and clouds of cooling gasses that showed where even more ships had vanished in thermonuclear annihilation.

Well beyond that battlefield were strewn other bits of wreckage and cooling gas. A long line of that flotsam stretched from halfway across the system to the neutron star. Sharing the orbit of the burned-out planet with the exhausted battle fleet was what appeared to be a bashed in demi-moon.

Every once in a while, a battlecruiser would make a minor adjustment to its orbit to stay clear of that thing.

"What the hell went on here?" her ops chief whispered.

"One hell of a brawl, Mondi, one hell of a brawl" Sandy said. Then, shaking herself, she turned to Comm.

"Send to Admiral Kitano. 'Grand Admiral Santiago sends her complements on a battle well fought and very well won. I bring you reaction mass so you can get your cripples underway for Alwa and, if you please, your battleworthy ships underway in pursuit of the fleeing aliens.' Comm, append our likely arrival time and send."

There was only a brief pause, before Comm answered, "It's on its way, ma'am."

"Very good. Now we wait."

That was the main trouble with space travel. You spent most of it waiting. Waiting for ships to arrive. Waiting for communications to be exchanged. Waiting.

Sandy settled in to wait for her message to get to Kitano and her reply to get back. Meanwhile, desperate crew members, maybe injured, or maybe in survival pods that had suffered damage, waited, fearing any breath could be their last.

In the débris field, activity had already begun. The thing about Smart Metal™ was that three or four survival pods didn't have to stay separate. Moving about the field were ships' longboats, collecting pods and merging them into themselves, growing as they went. As some of the pods flashing red were collected by their shipmates, the longboat's beeper might switch it off. Other times, the rescue boat's beeper would switch to red or even a flashing red.

There was only so much help that a longboat could provide a wounded sailor.

Sandy watched the story of desperate need and succor play out, helpless to do anything.

Of course, Kris Longknife inevitably provided her with a distraction.

Mondi asked her for a quiet talk in her night quarters. Once the door was shut, her operations officer blurted out, "Have you heard about the Alwa Station's Fraternization Policy?"

"Its what policy?"

"I'll take that as a no."

"If it involves fraternization, take that as a hell no."

Mondi took a deep breath. "Admiral, with Van left behind, the ship skippers have come to me as a stand-in chief of staff, and they may or may not have a problem."

"Mondi, you don't normally beat around the bush. What is it?"

The Navy officer raised her wrist, where her commlink rode. "You know we can program this Smart Metal to make our bed more comfortable, chairs, and the like."

"Yes."

"Supply makes entire walls disappear when they're moving crates around."

"Is there any content in all these words, Captain?"

"Our people weren't ashore very long before we sailed out for here, Admiral, but it was long enough for some of our hands to talk with Alwa Sailors. On Kris's fleet, ship's personnel are making walls disappear between their quarters."

"I'm not getting what you're telling me, Captain."

"Sailors who like each other are swapping their staterooms around to get next door to each other, then they're making the bulkhead between them go away doubling their living space."

"That sounds like a fine idea."

"They're also swapping bunks for double beds, queen size, double king size, depending on how many bulkheads they've made vanish."

Finally, the light dawned on Sandy. "Oh, shit. That Longknife girl hasn't done that to my Navy."

"It's standard Alwa policy."

Sandy rolled her eyes at the overhead, a silent prayer to any bureaucratic god listening.

"I was surprised to find her married. At least I hoped she was married, what with her bulging and very pregnant. Official policy, though?"

"One of our skippers actually messaged one of the Alwa ships that came out with us. I've got the official policy, if you want to see it."

Sandy did, and words began to stream across her own commlink.

"Kris Longknife did this!"

"Not by herself, Admiral. Sailors figured out how to make bulkheads go away on their own. Faced with an app she couldn't control and a fleet with no base force, she dumped the problem on the leading chiefs and XO's. They knocked the policy together while pulling an all-nighter. It's been modified a few times."

"But not changed."

"No, ma'am."

Sandy continued scanning the policy, but her mind was already racing through the problem and its ramifications. Her crews were young, eager, and far from home. Even her older officers were more than likely to be getting as far away from a domestic breakup as the galaxy allowed. Talk about foot loose, fancyfree . . . and horny.

"Do any of the skippers think that some of *our* Sailors have begun applying this app and the policy in advance of *my* authorization?"

"They haven't had any show up during quarters inspection, ma'am."

"*Scheduled* quarters inspection."

"Yes, ma'am."

When Ray Longknife had ordered Sandy out to Alwa Station he'd said the place was critical to keeping the alien monsters busy away from human space. He'd said the situation would, no doubt, be difficult.

Ray, you don't know the half of it.

"Computer, get me a chair. No, make that two," she said, waving Mandi at the first one to emerge from the deck. She settled into the next one, then leaned back and stared hard at the overhead.

"I now command the fleet on Alwa Station, correct?"

"That *is* what you read in your orders when you took command, Admiral."

Sandy saw where that would take her, and decided to avoid it for a few more minutes. "What other rumors did our talkative shore parties pick up in the short time they had to yak?"

Mandi took her time composing an answer. When it came, it was a whopper.

"The Sailors and Marines can get land grants down on the planet. They can go in with a few or a lot together and own a share of a farm, ranch, or hunting shack. The Alwans are handing out land grants, or maybe not deeds, but land use permits. Kris Longknife is making sure we don't steal the natives' land."

Sandy took that in and had a flashback to the bucket of snakes that the Pipra gal had dropped in her lap. No way would Kris let some money grabbing types strip plants from a river in native territory.

I've got to remember to be there when Kris gets her hooks into those dreamers.

As fun as that thought was, Sandy had this new hot potato to deal with. Call it a hot sweet potato.

Sandy had been a widow for a long time. She did have some old friends that she might occasionally go away with for a long weekend. She'd accepted that her command of a forlorn hope on the other side of the galaxy might very likely be on the celibate side.

She'd didn't exactly expect the same from her subordinates, but she'd assumed that rules were rules. Maybe she hadn't thought that through as far as she should have.

The preamble of Kris Longknife's fraternization policy put it bluntly. "We are here and not likely to be going anyplace soon. We also lack any shore facilities that might allow for the normal separation of intimate others," Sandy read aloud.

"Yes, ma'am," Mondi said.

"Do they have much of a shore facility now?" Sandy asked herself.

"I did get a readout of the base force, Admiral, before we sailed."

"And?"

"Yards and docks have mostly a highly skilled civilian workforce. No slots for sailors there. Supply needs people. It's growing as the fleet grows. But most of the workers are Colonial or Alwans, not a lot of slots for sailors. The only real place with underused personnel is what passes for a penal colony shoveling bird shit."

"Who's shoveling bird shit?"

Mondi had a quick answer for that one. "The two folks that sabotaged Kris's birth control implants resulting in her pregnancy. There also some sailors and Marines, including a few senior officers and chiefs that didn't take no for a no from a subordinate."

"So there are still a few teeth in this Longknife shacking up policy?" Sandy spat.

"There have been a lot of weddings," Mondi answered. "Still, some of the larger combinations don't seem to fit the usual requirements for a marriage license."

Sandy scowled at that, but Mondi didn't flinch.

"You wouldn't happen to know how this policy is working out, would you?"

"Admiral Hart said they've issued some warnings, admonishments, and reprimands to those who have a problem with the word 'no' that didn't go so far as to earn a shovel. At least yet. He said they'd also had to shuffle a few folks around the fleet after breakups that got nasty. Apparently, they've also added an approval system for when Cupid's arrow strikes too far up or down the chain of command. I'm told that Admiral Kitano herself has an ongoing relationship with the commander leading the engineering division of her flag, left over from when she was its skipper. Overall, the chiefs and the XO's have managed to make it work."

"Suddenly, you know a hell of a lot about this abomination."

"I'm the one that contacted Admiral Hart, ma'am. We've shot a couple of messages back and forth."

"Okay, Captain, do you have a recommendation?"

"Since you used the word abomination with reference to

said policy, I take it that after thirty-seven years in the Navy, you have a strong opinion."

"Very strong."

"I also know you to be a very flexible officer. Always on the lookout for a better way of doing things. Fixing what's broke."

"Are you saying that the Navy's Fraternization Policy is broke?"

"I'm saying we've walked off the edge of the world we know and we've got a whole lot of nothing to go on, ma'am. I'm also saying that you'll have a very difficult time walking the rest of the fleet back to the traditional way of doing things. Secondly, I don't see any way that you can allow the rest of the fleet to shack up and tell the new arrivals to suck it up, ma'am."

"You put my problem to me, succinctly. Oh, the sorrow of it," Sandy said with a sigh. "I come out here expecting to finally get my ass in a decent battle. I find Kris Longknife has smashed the hell out of the opposition and I'm stuck figuring out how to keep this lash-up together all by our lonesome on the other side of the galaxy. Hell, damn, spit," she said. She knew much more forceful words, but they failed her just now.

"Yes, ma'am."

"Okay, my ever-vigilant Ops Officer, I assume you have some recommendations for me before you brought me this steaming pile of shit."

"Yes, ma'am."

"And they are?"

"I'd suggest that you distribute the policy for comment to all skippers, XO's and leading chiefs and require their comments on the policy as well as any steps they might need to take to implement the policy if you should order it, Admiral."

"So, dump this ugly problem in the laps of those that will have to live with it, huh?"

"Yes, ma'am."

Sandy considered that. No doubt, Kris Longknife and her castaways had had more time to experience the problem of isolation on their Sailors before the extent of the abomination had raised its ugly head and they had to come up with a solution. Sandy could delay, and see what happened, but delay might lead to some real train wrecks as a few of her more rigid officers ran smack into some of her more creative Sailors.

Strange how I didn't think of that the other way around.

"Okay, Mondi, ask for comments. Give them three days to reply. We'll let this simmer for a bit."

"In the meantime, do you have any recommendations to your skippers about no-notice quarters inspections?"

"Yeah, tell them to stuff the idea and keep their eyes on the ball. We may be in a fight any minute. I don't want anyone creating problems I don't need."

"And the sailors?"

"Sailors were invented to create problems for officers, Mondi. It's just what they do."

4

At least the distant Kris Longknife created no more new problems for Sandy for the rest of that day. She got in a good supper and part of a good night's sleep before she was awoken by the duty orderly.

"Begging the Admiral's pardon, but we're getting a message from the battle fleet."

"I'm on my way," Sandy growled. In a moment, she'd splashed some water on her face and pulled on a fresh ship-suit. It was only a few steps from her night quarters, through her day quarters to her flag bridge.

On the main screen, a bedraggled woman's face was frozen in mid word. "Comm, let's hear what she has to say."

The screen went active.

"Kris, thank God you're back. We're down to using waste water for reaction mass when we have to dodge the wreckage of that last mother ship. I've got three pinnaces taking a slow trip to the nearest gas giant for reaction mass, but . . . oh, Admiral Santiago. It's you and not Kris. Sorry, ma'am, I just assumed. Did Kris make it back in time to stop that last batch of alien warships? Oops, you'll answer that in tomorrow's message. Don't get me wrong, I'm grateful for you showing up with fuel. As I was saying, we've got three pinnaces making a fuel run, and we'd use that to send more out to get more fuel. Still, we were faced with an awful slow recovery time and God only knows if those bastards have more ships. We're sitting ducks just now and I hate looking like duck soup."

Admiral Kitano glanced off screen, seemed to like what she saw and sighed. "I see that you've got Admiral Hart going pedal to the metal for our survivors. The fight was just too fast and too hard for me to leave even one ship behind to pick them up. We did drop off some longboats to help those that had gotten way from the wrecks. Still, it's been heart-breaking watching pods go from flashing red to silent. Godspeed to you, Admiral Hart."

Kitano took a deep breath, then squared her shoulders and reported, "About half my ships are too dinged or busted to risk in any kind of a donnybrook. They could put up a fight if they had to, but I'd rather they didn't. I intend to organize them into an escort force for the two beam ships here and have some of the better ones chase down the other beam ship that had to make a run for it. I'll handle all that. Once we've got fuel, I'm prepared to reshuffle, say sixty ships, into Miyoshi's Second Fleet and Bethea's Third. Then we can get a move on to see if there are any surviving bug-eyed monsters we need to chase down. I'd offer you our most combat experienced admiral, ma'am, but Admiral Hawkings collapsed with a coronary soon after the battle and he's in intensive care. We can talk more about this in your next messages."

Kris Longknife's deputy took another deep breath and let it out slowly. "I can't tell you how relieved I am to see you. We'll be waiting for you when you get here."

Sandy ran the message a second time, then did a check with sensors. They had identified the three objects making slow passage to the nearest gas giant as wreckage. Now, marked as human vessels, they were plotted and tracked. They'd likely make two trips out and back before Sandy's fleet got there.

Sandy went back to bed with more to mull over.

The next day, Admiral Hart began his rescue mission. He tasked some battlecruisers to slow early and start at one end of the debris field. Other ships delayed their deceleration by intervals so they could reach for those scattered along the length of the battlefield. Still, it was heart breaking the number of times a survival pod beeper went off line just as a rescue vessel heaved alongside.

Tear-jerking frustration.

"Aren't there any survival pods from the enemy?" a young second class on comm asked her chief.

The chief glanced around for an answer.

Had no one read any of Kris Longknife's reports on these monsters? Sandy thought to herself.

When no one else provided an answer, she said, "They don't surrender. They don't have survival pods and they don't evacuate their ships to lifeboats."

The young woman looked stricken at the answer. The older chief didn't look all that better. A lot of the crew around the bridge tightened the seat belts on their high gee stations and checked the button that would turn them into survival pods in a second and eject them from the ship a moment later.

Humans wanted, indeed, humans needed hope. What was missing in the soul of the enemy that it refused to grasp every moment of life?

Hart did his job, pulling desperate humans back from

the brink of the abyss. Battlecruisers and pinnaces moved through the scattered wreckage of ships and pulled men and women aboard. Many were grateful for a decent breath. Others were in greater need. Badly injured were triaged and shuttled from pinnace to battlecruiser for better care. All too soon, Admiral Hart was on the line.

"Admiral Santiago, I know I should be asking your permission for this, but by the time this message gets to you and your answer gets back to me, much of a day will be dead and gone, and with it some fine Sailors. I'm collecting the most seriously wounded on four of my ships. I'm ordering them back to Alwa for better care. I'll join you with the eight I have left."

Sandy eyed the screen. Admiral Hart was a short man, graying, and sporting a bit of a paunch. She had no idea what blend of hard work and chance had brought him to this point in his life, commanding a small task force and making the hard calls.

She smiled. He'd made the call, and was ready to take the consequences if this new elephant wanted to put pursuit of the enemy ahead of care for her own Sailor.

He'd made the right call.

"Admiral Hart, I concur with your detachment of a division for medical emergency purposes. Join me as soon as your rescue efforts permit."

The tension in the atmosphere on the *Victory's* bridge dissipated as the order went out. Admiral Hart wasn't the only one wondering what the new admiral was made of.

A day later, the *Victory* drifted up to Admiral Kitano's battle fleet. Battle damage was not all that noticeable; Smart Metal™ allowed for the most obvious outer damage to be smoothed over. Still, one of the spherical beam ships looked like someone had bashed it in with a giant's hammer.

To Sandy, the battle fleet presented a problem. She'd read in one of Kris's reports on the great voyage of galactic circumnavigation that they'd come up with a neat trick of mooring ships nose to nose and then swinging then around each other, thus getting a critically needed sense of down. Admiral Kitano's ships had used about their last bit of reaction mass to maneuver themselves into pairs and anchor together.

How could a pair of swinging ships take on reaction mass from a pinnace?

Sandy hailed Kitano. "I'm about to spawn sixteen pinnaces. Any suggestion as to how your ships refuel?"

"This won't be a problem," the other admiral replied. "Nelly developed an app for this. We'll let you know which of the two ships is the lightest and have your pinnace come along side it. Then we can pass a fuel line across to the other ship and refuel both of them together. That way, I should have thirty-two ships ready to fight or head off for the nearest gas bag in a couple of hours. There will be more later as you refuel them."

"We will conform to you," Sandy replied, and had Mondi issue the orders. Soon, sixteen pinnaces were being guided into sixteen pairs of ships. The docking quickly turned into a merging followed by huge lines being passed from the refueled ship up to the other. Even Sandy was amazed at how quickly the first thirty-two were refueled and the pinnaces detached.

The refueling was hardly completed before the refueled ships did a breaking burn, dropped down to skim the planet, and took off for the nearest gas giant, quickly accelerating to a good 2.5 gees.

While that was underway, Admiral Amber Kitano reported to Sandy's bridge.

"That's a smart bit of ship handling," Sandy said, pointing at the main screen, where a quarter or so of Amber's fleet was finishing up its refueling.

"It's an app Nelly developed for us," Admiral Amber Kitano said. "We were having a devil of a time getting ships all balanced out so we could moor them together. Trust Kris's Nelly to figure out a way to anchor ships together when we're off balance and weigh in differently."

"Nelly, you say? I suspect we'll really miss Kris's computer when she leaves," Sandy said.

"Leaves?" the other admiral asked, eyebrow raising.

"King Raymond has ordered her home."

"Why ever for?" Amber asked.

"He just gave me orders to relieve her, not explain it," Sandy said.

"Ours not to reason why, huh?"

"The usual."

"So, ah . . ." the young admiral seemed at a loss for words. "Will Kris's temporary promotions be rescinded?"

That stopped Sandy in her tracks. Since she arrived she'd observed the organization of the Alwa forces into a lot of fleets and task forces. References to admirals and commodores had been made with no doubt attached to them.

Now it was her turn to echo, "Rescind?"

"I don't think anyone out here has an official rank higher than commander. I know I don't. All of your senior commanders have been fleeted up from frigate skippers over the last year or so. Maybe in just the last few months as slots opened up and the need arose. We've got lieutenant commanders who came out in charge of gunnery or engineering holding down skipper slots."

Like a good staff officer, Mondi stepped in to give her

boss time to recover. "You mean that Admiral Hart, who totally intimidated us with ship handling that demonstrated how much we needed to learn real fast to jinks and dodge around, is a jumped-up frigate skipper?"

"Actually, Hart came out here as a retired commander assigned to yards and dock to help Admiral Benson run Canopus Docks. I think he was his deputy before Ben promoted him up to run the station when he was made boss of the base force. Hart was tickled to death to have command of a ship during the First Battle of Alwa, and then to be flagged up to command a task force."

"Alwa Station," Sandy said softly, trying not to make it sound derogatory.

"Yes, Admiral, promotions come quickly out here," Amber said. "They come quickly or you die real dead."

Sandy realized that being the new Grand Admiral in town out here might not have quite the authoritative kick it would have back home. Alwa was different. Lurking alien monsters. Fraternizing policy. Promotion policy. That was a whale of a lot of different to throw at a new boss woman.

Oh, and while you're figuring out what to do about Kris Longknife's unique way of running things, there's a batch of aliens running like mad for their uncles and aunts and cousins. Running with the latest news on how humans had once again kicked their butts way out of the ball park.

Sandy decided to ignore everything that wasn't critical for the moment. "Okay, how fast can we get underway and chase the aliens that snuck out the back door?"

Amber had brought her own Chief of Operations, Mike Unhof. She nodded to him and he stepped to the main screen and held his wrist unit up to it. The screen quickly turned into a map of the crazy system.

"We settled in with the neutron star. They had the better

two stars over on their side of this crazy system. We've got only one minor gas giant to refuel from. They've got a couple over there along with some serious rocks. They put all of them to good use building ships: speedsters as well as the door knockers. We'd never seen either of those before."

A list of ships cascaded down the side of the screen. "For now, we propose to reform the Battle Fleet into 1st and 2nd Battle Fleets. Or, if you prefer, Bat Fleet and Crip Fleet."

A scowl from Admiral Kitano brought a cough from her ops chief.

"Or Escort Battle Fleet, if you prefer."

"I do," Kitano growled. "Your sense of humor, Mike, will get you booted from my staff someday."

The briefer brightened at that threat, then continued. "We've shuffled the lessser damaged ships into Admiral Miyoshi's Second Fleet, which is refueling as we speak, and Admiral Bethea's Third, which is next. After each fleet is refueled here, we recommend they be detached to make a refueling pass at the nearest gas giant, then steer a high acceleration course for the huge gas bag nearest the jump the alien survivors fled through. They can top themselves off. We'd then order Miyoshi to take a peek through the jump. We've been ambushing the alien ships as they come through. They just might be ready to do the same to us. If the jump isn't guarded, he can take his fleet through and try to sniff out a trail to whatever jump they used, and head for it immediately. Race to it, stop, peek, jump through, repeat until we either catch them, lose the trail, or run into an ambush."

"And if we find an ambush?" Sandy asked.

The briefer turned to his boss. Admiral Kitano turned in her chair to face Sandy.

"That will depend on how big the ambush is. One of

those huge alien warships has two hundred or more lasers. We've spent the last five years staying out of range of one of those bastards. If they got our range, we'll be toast. If several of them got our range, I doubt even our crystal armor could handle the overload. Now, we've never gotten a good signature off one of those door knockers. What we know is that they got lots and lots of armor, rock, steel, water, all laid on real thick. Their reactors are fewer and farther between, likely to reduce the chance of them going off in a daisy chain. They also seem to have a longer-ranged laser, though just how many, we aren't sure. They don't seem to be built to a single pattern like the rest of the alien ships."

Kitano paused for a moment, gathered her thoughts, and went on. "If there are a dozen or more of those mothers waiting for us up close to a jump, Admiral, I can't recommend that we take the jump."

"What would you recommend?" Sandy asked.

"One of two options. We either pack up and go home, or we try to wait them out."

"We might figure a way around them," her ops chief offered. "Use some of the fuzzy jumps to get around them and come at them through another jump. Maybe drive them back through the jump we're waiting at or chase them down as they run for another jump."

"Have you done that before?" Sandy asked.

"Not really," Amber said. "So long as we don't tip them off that fuzzy jumps exist, it might be fun. But let's remember, a stern chase is a long chase. We have to remember that while we've got the two best fleets out here, who's protecting Alwa? The lame, sick and broken."

"And the new arrivals," Sandy put in. "I left forty-eight ships tied up at Canopus Station. Ben's running them through the yard to slap crystal armor on them."

"You're already up armored, right?" Amber asked.

Sandy shook her head.

"Oh, shit. We'll have to treat your task force like a bunch of eggshells."

"That bad?" Mondi asked to save her boss the embarrassment.

"One on one, they're toast. Two to one, we're still okay. Three or four to one and it gets dicey. Without crystal armor, you stay out of their range and use your speed to keep them where you want them."

"Very good," Sandy said, summing up what she'd learned since jumping into Kris's Longknife's command. She stood, and those around her did likewise. "We dodge, we weave, and we keep them at arm's length wherever and whenever possible. Mondi, Mike, cut us some operational orders to sign. Admiral Kitano, I am taking command of the Battle Fleet and the Escort Fleet. Please assign Admiral Drago to command the Escort Fleet to return all damaged ships to Alwa. You, Admiral Kitano, will command the Battle Fleet in pursuit of the alien fugitives. In doing this, you will be guided by the principle of calculated risk. The survival of Alwa depends on the continued existence of your Battle Fleet. Risk it in battle with the aliens when the prospects for success are high and losses are acceptable."

"Aye, aye, Admiral," Admiral Kitano said.

"Now let's go stop some aliens from telling their tale of what happened here."

5

G rand Admiral Sandy Santiago's *Victory* led her two battle squadrons through the jump. During the high gee chase across System X and the next system out, she'd managed to catch up with Admiral Kitano and Rear Admiral Bethea's 3rd Fleet. She and Rear Admiral Harts' collection of eight battlecruisers formed an *ad hoc* third task force to 3rd Fleet.

A bit less than a light hour away, Rear Admiral Miyoshi's 2nd Fleet was decelerating toward the nearest jump. One ship was already coasting to a stop in front of it. No doubt, this hard-driving scout would soon have a report on what lay beyond.

Ahead of Sandy, Bethea's thirty-two battlecruisers were already jacking their acceleration back up to the grueling 3.5 gees they'd used to speed them across one entire system and part of another. At least whoever had built the jumps had arranged for these two to be close together.

It took sensors a while, but they finally reported on the system. "We're in a system with a single yellow dwarf and six planets. Two of them are gas giants. There's a third jump all the way on the other side of the system. There's also a fuzzy jump a light hour away, but in the opposite direction from the one Admiral Miyoshi is checking out."

"Thank you," Sandy said, and settled back into her high gee station ready for another long wait.

A little over two hours later, Vice Admiral Kitano's intense face filled half of the main screen. Vice Admiral Bethea took up the other half.

"Admiral Miyoshi has found the enemy," Kitano reported. "At least some of them. A third window opened on the screen. The video was of poor quality, but three dozen ships could be seen, half-floating one hundred thousand kilometers in front of the jump. The others lurked behind it.

"Any way we enter that system, eighteen alien warships will have hundreds of lasers ready to sear our engines and reactors," Kitano said. "Thirty-six of the door knockers are there, and we will have to go through the jump one at a time."

Sandy well knew the physics. One jump. One ship. You could jam them through quickly, but warships needed space between them or they started doing more damage to themselves than the enemy ever could.

Well, maybe not this enemy, but enough to piss off the tax payers.

"Thirty-six, you say," Sandy said. "So, the other seventy-two or more are still running."

"While these play Horatio at the bridge," Kitano said.

"I wonder how long they'll hold here?" Bethea asked.

"I would imagine for a very long time," Kitano answered. "If you had drawn the short straw, would you quit your station before you had bought every possible minute that you could for your friends to escape?"

Bethea winced. "We don't know that any of these aliens

consider anyone their friends. Siblings, yes, but they are very competitive among themselves. Kris Longknife found that out when she discovered their home world. They like to brag about the planets they've sanitized of all life and jab anyone who's lagging."

That cast a pall over the discussion for a long moment as all three admirals mulled the critical need that these aliens must die or they would kill every last human in the galaxy.

"Okay," Sandy said, "we can't storm that jump from this end. I don't want to go home and let them win this one by just being obnoxious, so what other options do we have?"

"Navigator," Bethea said, glancing off screen, "where does that fuzzy jump take us?"

"On a wild round-about, ma'am, but five jumps would bring us back to the second jump into the system where they are barring the door against us."

"How long a wild round-about?" Sandy asked.

"A week at least," Kitano's flag navigator said.

That gave everyone pause. It was Admiral Kitano who began the new conversation.

"Admiral Drago is moving what's left of the 1st and 4th Fleets back to Alwa, as well as the beam ships. That's bound to take some time, and when they get back, they'll need more time to mend and fix ships. Hart, what kind of shape were the rest of Benson's Reserve Fleet in when you finished with the last of the aliens' forlorn hope?"

"Not badly dinged up, ma'am. We were close-hauled to the enemy as we closed on the same jump, but we pretty much got them before they got a good twist on us."

"So, twelve battlecruisers, all in reserve by now," Vice Admiral Betty Bethea summed up.

"Make that sixteen in reserve, Betty," Admiral Hart said. "The four I sent back with the wounded had a lot of my industrial and dock hands. They'll be back at work by now."

"We do have my newly arrived forty-eight ships," Sandy put in. "By now, some of them must have been up-armored."

"So, we've got sixty-four battlecruisers," Admiral Kitano went on, "some up-armored, some not, but all defending Alwa with another fifty plus damaged ships in need of serious yard time, plus the three beam ships, all in desperate need of a major refit."

"More like rebuilding," Betty put in.

"Meanwhile," Kitano said, "we've wiped out six alien mother ships and close to two thousand ships of one sort or another. Have we sanitized this chunk of space for Alwa?"

"Or is there some Johnny-come-late-to-the-party out there, headed for Alwa right now?" Admiral Hart put in.

"If he is out there, he'll have to pass through our warning buoys. We've picketed the Alwa System for the next twelve jumps out," Kitano pointed out.

"Assuming our picket line is still intact," Bethea put in. "The wolf packs we just kicked to the side of the road were taking our pickets out whenever they could."

Admiral Kitano was shaking her head. "Okay, yes, we've got problems, but when haven't we had a ton of problems on Alwa Station? Let me put it to you easy. Who here wants to go back to Alwa and tell Kris Longknife that we gave up and let all these door knockers get away without a fight?" The experienced Alwa admiral glanced around at the figures on her own forward screen, then shook her head.

"I'd rather have an eight-month-pregnant Kris Longknife biting the heads off of some alien wolf pack stupid enough to make a pass at her just now, than have her taking my head off."

"Seriously?" Sandy asked.

Kitano just eyed Sandy. On screen, Admiral Bethea looked away.

Sandy weighed all the information that had been dumped on her in the last few minutes. Even after dismissing the idea that some folks out here thought Kris might take a head or two, there was still a lot to absorb.

When she gave Kitano the command, Sandy had ordered her to apply calculated risk to this situation. How would *she* calculate the risk now? Alwa had some sixty to a hundred ships, some with more fight in them than others. They also had three beam ships that between them might have the fight of one. Commanding Alwa's forces was one very pregnant Kris Longknife. She'd taken down eight base ships, another wasn't likely to break her stride.

No, getting these doorknocker ships and the knowledge they had of how Kris had fought the last battle and beat them like a drum, was essential.

"We'll use the round-about route," Sandy said, "to get some ships into that system and pull the alien ships away from the jump. Once they start to run, the rest of you can jump through and cut them down at your leisure."

"But how many go and how many stay?" Kitano asked.

"If they break for the exit as soon as they see they've been outflanked, it would be better if both fleets were ready to pursue," Sandy said. "My task force is the closest to the jump and we don't have all that acceleration on the boats. Our twenty-four ships ought to be enough to get them running for the exit."

"And if they don't run?" Kitano said. "If they just hunker down at the jump and dare your puny twenty-four to tackle their thirty-six?"

"Remember, Admiral Santiago," Hart put in, "only my eight battlecruisers have the crystal armor."

"That's a bridge we'll blow up when we come to it," Admiral Santiago said. "Admiral Kitano, you take command of 2nd and 3rd Fleets on this side of the jump. If Bethea will have her navigator transfer his proposed course to my navigator, we'll get this diversion underway."

Two minutes later, Sandy's Diversion Task Force had its course and orders to go to four gees. Very rapidly, Bethea's forces fell behind as Sandy hurtled toward her first battle with these vicious aliens Kris Longknife had stumbled upon.

Six and a half grueling days and five huge jumps later, Sandy's *Victory* led the Diversion Task Force through its final jump into the system where a two-day high gee charge would put them at the throat of alien rock mounds with thermonuclear reactors and more lasers that any generous god should have allowed.

It took Sensors only a moment to report that nothing appeared to have changed since they got their last report from Vice Admiral Miyoshi just before they began their wild ride around the enemy flank.

It would be several hours before Sandy knew the enemy's reaction to her arrival, so she gave the order to accelerate toward the enemy at four gees and then, according to her schedule, she went to sleep.

She awoke seven and a half hours later, a good half hour before her orderly would have called for her. Since the duty watch had let her sleep, she suspected strongly that they were in no danger.

A glance at the main board as she motored her high gee

station onto the flag bridge showed her that she was both correct and incorrect.

She was in no immediate danger; the aliens were nowhere nearby. No, that was not the problem. The problem was that during her entire night's sleep the aliens had not budged from their attack position, guarding the jump that Sandy really wanted to lure them away from so Kitano and her two fleets could jump through and start annihilating them. Eighteen heavily gunned rock piles still held formation a hundred thousand klicks from the front of the jump. The same number stood guard at the rear of it.

She was a diversion charging down on an enemy that appeared to be impervious to her distraction.

While she considered her problem, she had Comm call up Admiral Hart. "We seem to be a failure as a scarecrow," she said.

"Don't you hate it when the bad guys turn out to be smart sons of bitches," was his reply.

"Have they fought like this before?" Sandy asked.

"We've caught them a couple of times trying to slip away from a jump that we'd fought over and held when they tried to force it. They may have had a distant observer to the massacres that ensued. Or it could just be that these guys are here to delay us and they're going to delay us for all they're worth. Besides, us fighting twenty-four is a whole lot better than fighting a whole lot more."

"Maybe I should have balanced our forces better," Sandy concluded, realizing she had misjudged the temper of her enemy.

We live and learn. If we live on Alwa Station

"We live and learn, ma'am," Admiral Hart said, as if he'd read her mind.

"Any suggestions?" she asked. It was past time to beg,

steal or borrow any advice she could get from an old
Alwa hand.

"You probably already know this, but I'd come up on
them a bit on the slow side. If we're still hard charging and
braking at four gees, they could charge out at us and we
wouldn't have anything left in the engines to dodge out of
range. Whatever we do, your ships have got to keep them at
arm's length. Hell, ma'am, I want to keep my ships at arm's
length. That crystal armor is nice, but if we get pinned by a
hundred lasers or more, it's bound to get hot in here."

Sandy liked the jumped-up commander's sense of
humor as well as his keen insight. It had been a long peace.
Hell, her only fight had been holding Kris Longknife's coat
while her fast attack boats closed with those six huge
battlewagons of unspecified origin. No matter how many
stars on their collar, everyone from human space was a
novice.

Best to ask for advice from folks that have seen this
elephant. This very huge elephant.

Sandy cut the acceleration to 3.5 gees and started laying
on a long list of drills, tests, and weapons checks. She was
none too sure what the odds would be against her. If every
alien turned to take her on, they would have to expect a fleet
was waiting on the other side of the jump to cut them up.
No, only some of the alien ships would turn their attention
to her. Just how dangerous would these door knockers be?

Whatever the odds, it was bound to get wild real soon.

7

The *Victory* was in the final moments of a soft two gee deceleration; Sandy had aimed to bring her fleet dead in space 200,000 klicks short of the eighteen rock piles that held the front of the jump. They had their rock-armored noses aimed at the jump. Their vulnerable sterns were pointed away from it and directly at Sandy's fleet with its four hundred 22-inch lasers.

If nothing changed, this would be a very quick execution.

So, of course, the enemy changed their deployment.

Eight of the sixteen ships closest to Sandy flipped and headed for her at a 2.5 gees acceleration. Two hundred thousand klicks farther away, from the back side of the jump, eight of the sixteen also lit their rocket motors. They also accelerated for Sandy's ships at 2.5 gees. Sixteen heavily armored ships loaded with lasers accelerated at her with all they could get from their reactors.

"Comm, send to task force. "Up deceleration to four gees," Sandy ordered immediately. Fortunately, she had kept her ships at Condition Zed and her crews in their high gee

stations so they were ready to answer her orders immediately.

The aliens hurtled toward her ships, but her fleet
succeeded in coming dead in space and began their own
acceleration well before the aliens pulled within 200,000
klicks.

As soon as the aliens were in range of her big lasers,
Sandy ordered the aft batteries to open fire.

Her battlecruisers might as well have been throwing
snowballs for all the good it appeared to do.

"Flag to all ships, on my command, we will kill our
deceleration burn, flip ship, and empty all forward batteries
at once. All ships will concentrate on the closest ship and
aim for one specific point on its hull. I want to burn that
sucker bad."

She quickly got acknowledgments.

"Cease deceleration. Flip ship. Fire. As soon as you've
shot yourself empty, flip ship and lay on four gees."

There was a slight additional hum in the *Victory's* background noise, but no other evidence that the twelve lasers in
the forward battery were sucking the juice from twenty-four
huge capacitors and any other electricity the ship might
have available. Sandy ignored the sound of the flagship
around her and concentrated on the main screen.

The closest ship glowed red and streamed a mixture of
lava, gas and steam . . . but it did not explode.

Two other ships looked like they were also taking fire.
Apparently, the definition of the closest ship was more
ambiguous than Sandy intended.

The *Victory* shot itself dry, flipped and once again Sandy
felt the oppressive weight begin. Yes, the high gee stations
kept the acceleration from squashing her like a bug, but it

could not keep her from feeling just how heavy her body was.

The ships settled into a 2.7 gee acceleration. The aliens were accelerating slower, but they'd built up more momentum. Somewhere around 160,000 klicks they'd match the aliens. Then Sandy would have her ships pull back out to 200,000 klicks before matching acceleration.

Once the aft batteries were reloaded, Sandy concentrated the entire fleet on the most damaged alien ship.

This time, all twenty-four of her ships concentrated on a single alien ship.

Some laser burned through somewhere. A line of explosions swept through the targeted ship and its acceleration fell off drastically.

When Sandy's ships flipped to bring their bow lasers to bear, they slammed the same alien ship they'd been savaging. It was already hurting. Now they sliced into it and through it.

One moment it was there, then a terrible explosion started amidships and shot aft. In the blink of an eye, the aft half of the ship was gone and only an expanding cloud of superheated gas filled the space where it had been. The bow, like an obscenely ripped off head, shot off, tumbling in space.

Without an order, all of Sandy's ships ceased fire, retargeted their lasers to the next closest ship, and slammed it. Capacitors exhausted, fire ended, and the fleet flipped almost as one.

The fleet returned to its 2.7 gee acceleration. Now the range was back at 200,000 klicks. Sandy ordered her ships to match its flight to that of the onrushing charge of the enemy. The flips to fire the forward batteries would allow the enemy to gain on them, but only a bit. The battle was well under control.

Then *Formidable* began to fall behind.

"*Formidable*, report your status?" The order came from the *Formidable*'s squadron commander, but Sandy followed it intently.

"We have suffered an engineering casualty. Two of our reactors are off line. We can only make 2.3 gees on our remaining reactor."

All the ships from human space were new construction, tested and accepted. They'd made the run across the galaxy at 2.5 to 3.0 gees with only a few minor problems that had been fixed easily. Admittedly, Sandy had pushed them hard at 4.0 gees during this flanking run.

There was no way to tell what had failed or why.

Sandy shook it off. Her fleet had an engineering casualty on a major warship, and now it was up to her to factor that failure into her fight and adjust for it.

"Comm, send to all. Fleet acceleration is now 2.3 gees. Please advise flag on status of power plants."

The fleet slowed. Down the side of Sandy's main board now cascaded the name of all her ships and an indicator of their engineering status. Most were green. A few were yellow. Two were red. One was the *Formidable*. The other was the *Illustrious*.

"Comm, do we have a report from the *Illustrious* yet?"

"Coming in now, Admiral."

As she stared at her board, the voice of the *Illustrious*'s skipper reported. "We've pulled one reactor off line. As soon as it cools enough, we'll send bots inside to effect repairs. I wish they'd convert the reactors to Smart Metal, but they aren't, so we'll do this the old way. Out."

Two of her ships were limping. One was out of the fight

and could not maintain fleet speed. The other might be able to keep up with the fleet, but with only two of its three reactors on line, reloading its lasers would be slow.

After blowing away one enemy ship, Sandy had lost the use of twenty, maybe forty of her four hundred lasers.

The remaining twenty-two ships had just finished firing their aft batteries at the singled-out enemy ship. It was time to flip. While twenty-two ships ceased acceleration, flipped, and slashed at the closest alien rock pile, two battlecruisers continued their acceleration, pulling ahead of the rest of the human ships but continuing to lose ground against the onslaught of alien warships.

The target threw out jets of steam and red-hot lava. A chunk of something red hot was seen to fly off. Still, no matter how hurt it was, its commander kept his course and acceleration steady, aiming straight for the humans, closing the distance slowly but surely until it might bring its lasers to bear.

That ship did not survive the next iteration of the fire, flip, fire, flip.

The squadron redirected its fire onto the next alien ship to which the honor of being the closest fell. It took the honor with pure stoicism.

By the time they had dispatched it, the alien stone wagons were coming up on 175,000 klicks from the human battle line. Sandy had just finished firing her forward batteries and flipped back to accelerate when the aliens popped a surprise of their own.

8

I t shouldn't have been a surprise. Her ships had been concentrating their fire since the battle started, aiming for a single ship, a single spot on that single ship, doing their best to put the maximum energy into the smallest space.

Suddenly, the five remaining alien rock piles lit up with all their lasers. Close to a thousand lasers reached out, not for the ship closest to them, but the one that hadn't been firing the last couple of flips.

Formidable.

She had actually pulled ahead a bit, not losing time to flip and fire, but keeping up her acceleration even while Sandy's other ships were coasting and firing their forward batteries aft. Still, she was the ship the aliens chose to concentrate all their lasers on.

Lasers, by definition, are coherent light. A laser beam stays solid, concentrated, deadly. In an atmosphere, smoke, clouds, or even the atmosphere on a clear day can disperse the power of a beam, cause the concentration to bloom out and lose power as the distance stretches out.

Even in space, there is enough random gas in the so-called vacuum of space to bleed out the energy of a beam, to reflect part of it, to cause it to bloom and lose concentration. The alien lasers were something like the human 14-inch or 15-inch lasers. They were effective out to about 100,000 klicks.

The latest versions of the alien lasers seemed to have been fine tuned to reach out 120,000 klicks.

At 175,000 plus clicks, those lasers shouldn't have been good for much more than warming coffee.

However, if you take 800 or more lasers and concentrate them on one ship, you can do a lot more than warm coffee.

As the alien ships lit up, Sandy realized her mistake.

"All ships, Evasion Plan 3. Now."

She should have ordered it sooner. She should have expected something like this.

But the enemy wasn't firing.

Sandy shook away her excuse. She should have expected the unexpected.

Throughout her small fleet, captains struggled to mouth her orders, helm crews jumped to obey her voice or maybe their own captain, or maybe they saw the light from the distant ships and knew they had been complacent for way too long.

Sandy had her fleet arrayed in three lines by squadron, each ship showed its stern to the enemy as it matched acceleration with the aliens. One newly arrived squadron was above her own; Admiral Hart's scrimmage squadron was below. There were five thousand klicks between the ships, right, left, up and down.

The *Formidable* was the fifth ship in Sandy's squadron.

Her skipper made the right call.

He couldn't go any faster, but he could get the hell out of

the center of all those beams. He took off high and to his right, passing close aboard *Irascible*, but getting his vulnerable engines at least somewhat protected from the incoming fire.

Sandy ground her teeth but kept her mouth firmly shut; she would not request a report. That skipper would report when he damn well had the time.

Around her, while she had eyes only for the drama centered on the life or death struggle of the *Formidable*, the rest of the fleet dodged up and down, but more right or left, forcing a deflection shot on the enemy if they wanted a bite out of their vulnerable reactors.

"High and low BatRons, increase distance to ten thousand klicks from my squadron. Squadron commanders, increase the interval between ships to ten thousand klicks."

Her three subordinates answered with two flashes of their comm light.

It was coming up on time to return the favor with their aft batteries. The time to be fat, dumb, and happy was long gone.

"Admiral Hart, please have your two divisions divide their fire between the two right-most ships."

"Aye, aye, ma'am."

"BatRon 2, You will divide your fire by divisions between the two ships to the left."

"Aye, aye, Admiral."

"BatRon 1, you will concentrate on the central target." BatRon 1 was minus the *Formidable*. The *Illustrious* was only contributing half as many guns to each broadside. Time would tell how long it would take Sandy's squadron to destroy their target so that she could retarget them to concentrate on one of the other four.

Behind them, the enemy began to jinks a bit. What they

did was slow and jerky. It helped them miss a few salvoes, but the battlecruiser's fire was relentless and more likely to be spot on. Alien ships' bows glowed, spewed steam and boiling lava. Every once in a while, never often enough, their 22-inch laser fire was rewarded with a secondary explosion as their shots penetrated the armor and destroyed a laser or its capacitor. It would blow up, adding alien destruction to the human fire.

Sandy didn't know how long it would take the aliens to reload their lasers. She didn't know if they would hold their fire for another concentrated five-ship broadside or allow fire at will. As soon as the aft batteries were spent, Sandy flipped her fleet and fired a full salvo from her bow guns.

Through it all, the alien lasers stayed silent.

"When we flip ship, I want all ships to set a base course at forty-five degrees from the base course and three gees acceleration. *Formidable*, you may proceed independently."

She got an answer from her subordinate battle squadron commanders but from the *Formidable*, only silence.

Her lasers reached empty. "Flip ship. Adjust course and speed. Now."

Within their jinks pattern, her ships conformed to her orders.

Sandy studied what her sensors showed of the *Formidable*. She had continued a zig-zag climb until she was well above the top squadron. There was something different about her engines, but sensors couldn't give Sandy a solid picture.

Formidable picked that moment to urge an extra .2 gees out of her engines, then flipped her zig over ninety degrees to a definite zag.

That was when the aliens shot everything they had at her.

Some raked her broadside. Sandy could see steam streaming out from the hull where the lasers had sliced through the reflective Smart Metal^{TM} skin into the honeycomb beneath. That layer was filled with reaction mass for the express. It was intended to both ablate away some of the heat from laser hits but it also steamed out into space to disrupt the concentration of the incoming laser beam.

The armor worked as designed. The question was how much her engines were suffering.

The *Formidable's* skipper cut power and flipped his ship, bringing his bow armor to bear and protecting his vulnerable engines. He was fighting his ship, one against five, and doing all the desperate dance moves he could to stay alive.

Sandy tore her eyes away from the *Formidable*, and glanced down her entire battle array. While *Formidable* had eked out a few extra points of acceleration for his ship, Hart's ships were falling behind, allowing the enemy to close on them.

"Hart, would you care to explain your course change?"

"My Sapphire has got crystal on her hide, ma'am. All my squadron does. Your Formidable is in trouble. Out on Alwa Station, fixing or replacing ships is no problem. Finding crews for more ships is a bitch. Permission to steer closer to the enemy, Admiral."

"As you will, sir," Sandy allowed, which was a phrase she suspected she'd be using a lot on Alwa Station.

Who asks for orders to Alwa Station? she asked herself.

People as crazy as Kris Longknife, she answered.

The *Formidable* appeared to win this particular round with alien death. She was still maneuvering as the enemy lasers fell silent. As soon as they did, the skipper adjusted his course. He didn't quite end the dodging and weaving, but he did set his course as straight as he possibly could to put more distance between himself and his tormentors.

Twice more they repeated their strange evolution. The *Formidable* doing its wild jig with death while the other battlecruisers raked the five alien ships with three or four withering broadsides.

Sometime between two or three human salvos, the aliens did their best to catch the *Formidable* in a misstep. They failed, and she began to work her acceleration back up to 2.4 and finally 2.5 gees with accessional forays under fire to even 2.7.

Astern, the five alien ships began to stumble themselves. Sandy could not get a shot off at their vulnerable sterns, but her intense fire was slashing through the stony fortress these ships presented her.

Here and there, lasers blew, becoming momentary volcanoes spewing rock, lava and ice for a moment. Some of the damage must have reached aft to engineering spaces because two of ships began to slow. The first to fall off was the one Sandy was concentrating her squadron on, then one of Admiral Hart's targets faltered and fell behind.

Slowly, with bleeding fingers, the *Formidable* pulled ahead and the aliens fell behind.

However, the more these five fell behind, the closer they were to being joined by the eight ships that had started this long, stern chase two hundred thousand klicks further away. These were the ones from the far side of the jump. They had been lurking there, intent on shooting their hundreds of lasers up the tender sterns of Admiral Kitano's ships as they came through the jump.

Sandy very much needed to finish off these five before she had to tackle another eight.

The ship her reduced squadron had been concentrating

on suffered some sort of engineering casualty. It stumbled off in a straight line just as Sandy's forward batteries were about to exhaust their capacitors. Still, all seven of her ships got solid hits on their target for the last second of their volley.

Random explosions began to tear it apart.

Sandy quickly flipped her fleet and her squadron began to peel the enemy ship even as it came apart inside out from cascading explosions.

"Check fire. Check fire," Sandy ordered as the target suddenly vanished in a cloud of superheated gas.

"Switch fire," she ordered, "to Admiral Hart's weak target."

In only a moment, all of Sandy's ships joined Hart's four ships chipping away at the ship that was having the most trouble maintaining course and speed.

Two flips later, that alien ship couldn't stand the punishment any longer and blew into tiny pieces.

Sandy now concentrated a squadron of ships on each of the damaged aliens. The last of them was gone before the first of the alien eight came into what the humans had come to accept as their maximum range.

The *Formidable* chose that moment to announce its progress. "I've got the second reactor coming back on line. It's only giving me partial power, but I should be able to make three gees. I've rearranged my stern constructing small rocket engines and spread them over more space. I can maintain a fleet acceleration up to 3.2 gees."

"Fleet, acceleration 3.2 gees," Sandy ordered, allowing herself a wisp of a sigh. "Let's give them a blast from the stern chasers, shall we?"

Actually, she let the aft batteries carry the fight for a few minutes while they ran themselves well out of range of the onrushing aliens. That didn't stop the alien warships from firing even after they were well out of effective range, which only demonstrated how far out-ranged their guns were, compared to the 22-inch lasers on the battlecruisers.

Once Sandy had regained 195,000 klicks distance from the aliens, she returned to the previous drill. Fire, flip, fire, flip, reload.

Sandy also concentrated her entire fleet on one ship as a kind of test.

The grand admiral had read Kris's reports. The enemy never surrendered. The enemy fought to the last round and then opened their ships to vacuum for their final breath.

Sandy had read all those reports. Still, she couldn't believe them. She wanted, needed, to see it for herself.

The aliens showed her with full intent. They fought. They never stopped fighting. Only when the blast of human lasers burned them to gas did they cease the battle.

Never did Sandy's sensors spot a single longboat or survival pod separate from an alien warship. One small boat might have tried to get away, or maybe it just came loose. If it was a serious run for survival by someone, it was shot out of space by fifty of that ship's own lasers.

Surrender was not a word in their alien language and, as eight ships came under her fire, one at a time, all eight of them died. Not one swerved away from their end. Sandy was left with a sick feeling in the pit of her stomach.

This isn't war. This is murder.

Whatever it was, eight ships stayed in line and died with every living crew member still on board.

9

Sandy ordered her ships to one gee and dogged the watch. Half the crew would stay alert at their post while the other half got their first shower in way too many days to remember and maybe, if the mess crew could manage it, a real, honest to God hot meal. Two hours later, the clean and well-fed would take over the watch from the stinky and hungry, and they could get squared away and fed before returning to their station.

"Nav, I want a one gee course that will get us well back from that damn jump so we can take time to do some serious maintenance. If it confuses the aliens and leaves them thinking we're running for a jump, that's all the better. If there's a nearby gas giant, aiming us for that might rattle them even better."

"Yes, ma'am. The flag navigator worked his Ouija board for a long moment, then recommended a course and acceleration. Sandy passed it along to the comm, and the fleet conformed to her orders. With a sigh, she motored off the bridge, leaving it to Mondi to divide the bridge staff.

With creaking muscles, she pulled herself out of her

stinking high gee station, set it to self-clean, per the manual's promise, and headed for her own shower to clean the sweat and stink that the egg was supposed to have taken care of, but never did.

"The guy who actually comes up with a design for a high gee station," Sandy muttered to the shower head, "that really lets you bounce out of one of those torture machines smelling fresh as a daisy and feeling fit as a teenager will make a fortune."

She turned around to let the hot water splatter on the many knotted muscles in her back. "And I'll be in line to buy the first one."

Fifteen minutes later, in a clean ship suit and with only slightly mussed drying hair, she made her way to the *Victory's* senior officer's wardroom. The mess crew had outdone themselves. How they managed to have fresh bread ready left Sandy wondering if she shouldn't yank the mind reader or fortune teller from the mess deck's team and put them where she really needed them, at her elbow in flag plot.

The meatloaf might have shown evidence of defrosting, but the bread made up for it.

Fed with something that didn't come in a tube for the first time since she ordered her ships into an extended high gee run, Sandy returned to her room to find that the Smart Metal™ had done its miracle for the high gee station and returned it to pristine condition. She stripped out of her shipsuit, boarded and closed up the station, and headed back to the bridge.

She'd taken less than an hour, but when she offered to relieve Mondi, the captain refused.

"What are we going to do with the sixteen alien door knockers that we've got left?" she asked her admiral.

Sandy ran a worried hand through her wet hair. "It seems to me that they get a vote."

"Yeah," her ops chief muttered, gnawing on a cuticle. "As I see it, they have three options, none of them good. They can stay where they are. We drift up and shoot them to hell from outside their laser's range, and leave them dead without having fired a shot. I suspect that will be a non-starter."

Mondi seemed to discover the finger in her mouth, and switched to holding her hand out, two fingers up. "They can repeat what they just did, peeling four ships off of each side of the jump, chase us back a bit while dying, but buying time for the others to hold the jump a bit longer."

Sandy nodded. She suspected that would be the chosen strategy.

"Or they can come off their guard stance and charge us with all they've got, pushing us to see if they can get lucky and get a ship."

Sandy shook her head. "They'd have to know that there's someone lurking on the other side of that jump. Kitano would be on them like fleas on a dog."

"We're here, ma'am. They don't really know what's there, but yes, I'd bet on the second option. So I'd suggest we take our time, get some serious maintenance and repairs going on our ships, let the crew get a good night's sleep, and see what our aliens choose to do."

A day and a half later, Sandy's battle array drifted up to a spot in space 200,000 kilometers from the nearest alien rock mound. Lasers were loaded all around. Even the *Formidable* stood ready to fire half broadsides. They were ready to begin what looked to be a simple execution.

So the aliens chose that moment to demonstrate just how alien they were.

First, one ship blew up. One huge explosion started aft in engineering and shot through the ship. In the blink of an eye, there was nothing there but roiled superheated gases.

A second later, another ship performed its self-immolation. A third and fourth followed in the blink of an eye. The last four went out at two second intervals as if someone was calling cadence.

Before Sandy could pull in a shocked breath, the eight on the back side of the jump blew themselves up in a single explosion.

"Holy Mother of God..." Sandy breathed softly.

"...Help them," Mondi finished.

Sandy stared at the main screen as the roiling clouds of gas expanded and dissipated away into the vastness of space. Slowly she closed her mouth as the realization came to her that it was hanging open. Nothing in her life prepared her for what she had just witnessed.

Intellectually, she knew that her Navy service during the long peace left her unprepared to take over a fighting command from Admiral Kris Longknife. In her head, she knew she was coming out here to a command where combat was not just possible, but probable. Still, it was one thing to know that she might have to fight for her life and kill to save herself and others. It was something else entirely to see it, experience it not just in the head, but in the gut.

Sandy fingered the yellow and black striped handle that, with one pull, would convert her high gee station into a survival pod and send it hurdling into space. Every ship she'd served on came equipped with some sort of survival pod, none as fancy as Smart Metal™ allowed hers to be on the *Victory*. As a human being, she would fight for her life until her dying breath.

Her enemy had just proved to her just how alien they

were. Not just alien but completely opposite from us. *What could make someone do that?*

Sandy shook her head, as if to shake off a blow.

"Know thy enemy," had been hammered into her since her first day at the academy. She'd studied human differences through the ages and, under secure conditions, studied the differences that divided even the humans of the United Society, and, when that vanished away, had studied the capabilities and intents of several of the factions that fragmented humanity had splintered into.

Sandy thought she knew just how different her enemy might be.

But now she was on Alwa Station and her first look into the alien enemy's eyes had left her stunned by the difference between them.

Sandy set her jaw. "Clearly, I need to understand those bastards more than I do now," she said, half to herself.

"Yes, ma'am," Mondi agreed.

With a deep sigh, Sandy shook herself out of the dark cloud that befuddled her. This question would have to wait. She had a fleet to get back to where it belonged.

"Navigator, set a course for that jump. Let's take it easy through the jump. No need for us to risk a ship now that we are no longer under attack.

10

Sandy sent a warning buoy through the jump before she cautiously led her ships through. Admiral Kitano had her fleet moored well back, 150,000 klicks, each of her ships swinging around another, comfortably anchored.

"Did you see what they just did?" Sandy asked Kitano when the admiral came on line.

"Yeah. We've seen them fight like wildcats one minute, then give over to despair and suicide the next. They're crazy."

Sandy sighed. "I'm inclined to agree with you. When I headed out from Canopus Station, I wondered what a person of my paygrade was doing chasing around space, using her battlecruisers for tankers, then running off for some kind of personal fight. I think I needed to see this to actually believe what we're up against."

Kitano nodded. "You have to actually see these bastards in action to believe they can be this alien. The only thing I'd add to get you fully briefed up on conditions on Alwa Station would be a visit to that pyramid on the alien home planet. Maybe add a visit to the next planet over that they sterilized down to bedrock."

"I've seen Kris Longknife's report on both," Sandy said. "I really didn't want to smell the place or taste it up close and personal. I hoped to do without those nightmares. I'm starting to think I may have to do it."

"I would suggest it, Admiral. Now I would also suggest that we get back to Alwa. We've been gone over a month."

"Let's take it easy, say one gee, maybe 1.25 gees. I don't know about your ships, but mine need some serious love from a competent dockyard."

"Dockyards we've got on Alwa Station," Amber said, beaming. "Let's get your ships into them."

They had hardly gotten underway at a gentle 1.25 gee acceleration when Mondi was at Sandy's elbow. "Admiral, about that abominable policy of Kris Longknife's?"

Sandy raised a questioning eyebrow, pretty sure what would come next.

"Fifteen of your skippers request you immediately implement the policy. We've done some hard fighting and The Word is out below decks that a change is coming."

"And the one skipper who isn't asking?"

"Ma'am, he's chomping at the bit to do some no-notice quarters inspections. He's real sure his crew is already doing stuff against God and regulations."

"So if I don't do something, something is going to be done to me."

"I'm afraid so, ma'am. Not all the talk between ships has been to improve combat efficiency. Stories about victory celebrations in Admiral Hart's squadron have gotten around."

"Sailors are such gossips," Sandy muttered. "So I either follow Kris Longknife's policy or I risk all kinds of guff."

"Guff," Mondi coughed softly. "All kinds."

Sandy rolled her eyes at the overhead and took a deep breath. "Not for the first time, or the last, I suspect, I'm going to curse Kris Longknife's shadow. Issue the order. All newly arrived squadrons will adopt the Alwa Station Fraternization policy. May all the gods of sea and space have mercy on their fornicating souls."

"Yes, ma'am," Mondi said, and went to issue the order.

Three weeks later, the *Victory* arrived in the Alwa system via Jump Point Beta just in time to see the *Wasp*, with Princess Kris Longknife and one tiny princess Longknife, take the Alpha point for human space. What with all of Sandy's chasing aliens around space, Kris must have not only had her baby, but found her strong enough for the journey home.

Space is huge and human time ticks on.

The *Victory* was waved directly into a maintenance slipway rather than a pier.

Sandy hardly had a moment to settle behind her desk and begin to tackle more of the huge stack of reports that had been flooding into her inbox since *Victory* got in the Alwa system, than her yeoman announced, "Admiral Benson is here for you."

"And Granny Rita," came in a cranky voice that arrived only moments ahead of a tall, whip-thin woman of undetermined years, although her gray hair and the crinkles around her gray eyes showed she'd seen many miles go by. She held out her hand.

Sandy rose to accept it, puzzled at the woman who seemed to command the room even with herself, Admiral Benson, and now Pipra Armstrong trailing into the space.

"Granny Rita?" Sandy said, tasting the word.

"Once I was Rita Longknife, but it's been years since I

shared a bed with that scoundrel. I go by Granny Rita these days, and I've earned it."

A light went off in Sandy's head. "Commodore Longknife. The long-lost Commodore Rita Nuu-Longknife."

"I knew where I was the whole damn time, so you can forget that lost bit, and yes, I commanded BatCruRon 1 when we won our last battle, and, I hear, the war. I got chased so far and so fast for our effort, that we ended up all the way across the galaxy."

Sandy gulped, and found herself tearing up. "You knew my grandfather. You used your first pregnancy that day to help them get the bomb past security that he used to kill President Urm."

"Oh, God, you're one of our Santiagos," Rita said, and came around the desk to engulf Sandy in a hug. "I remember your grandfather. He was so handsome and so brave. He chose to take the bomb in. He chose to," she said, ending in a gentle whisper of awe.

And so the Longknife legend had begun on a lie, that Ray Longknife had assassinated President Urm of Unity and ended the war between the Rim's hundred and fifty worlds and Earth's fifty allied planets. The Longknifes and the Santiagos knew the truth, even if everyone else ignored it. The Longknifes and Santiagos had begun a relationship in which the Longknifes took and the Santiagos gave, often to that last measure.

Sandy shook her head. Ray Longknife had sent her here. Kris Longknife was dropping this uniquely crafted amalgamation of challenges and problems in her lap, and now she had Rita Nuu-Longknife, no matter what she called herself, standing in her office.

This couldn't be good.

Sandy wiped her eyes, took a step back and eyed Rita. "What ill wind brings you to my office?" she said cautiously.

The old woman took two steps back herself and resumed a more reserved stance. "I'm just trying to figure out what Ray might have told you about this place and what kind of portfolio you think he's handed off to you."

Sandy motioned Rita and the other two to chairs on the other side of her desk. She settled into her chair and ran through her orders in her mind.

"Clearly, I command all allied forces in the Alwa Defense Sector."

"Not the Alwa System?" Rita asked.

"Sector. Why?"

"Well," the elder stateswoman said, suddenly uncomfortable in her chair. "The system is pretty obvious. Sector might just be taken to include all the systems we're got automated outposts in to give us warning of any incoming trouble. Then again, it might include the Sasquan System. You know, the star system Kris Longknife stumbled across with cats that have their pretty little claws on nuclear triggers."

"Yeah, I heard about them," Sandy said, frowning. Had a Santiago once again been set up by a Longknife, even if he was now a royal Longknife?

Or was this woman, officially no longer a Longknife, doing her best to job her?

"What about the felines?" Sandy asked cautiously. Then added, "Do we actually call them felines?"

"They prefer to go by Sasquans, but their translators don't get upset with felines or even cats. Don't call them kittens to their face though," Ben put in.

"A diplomatic challenge, huh?" Sandy said.

"A challenge in several levels," Rita said. "We think we killed most of the aliens that know they're there, but you can never tell with those bastards for sure. The cats are now hell bent on getting into space. Do we help them? Does our help to them depend on them putting the thermonuclear genie back in the bottle, or do we ask them to stew up a batch of those atomic bombs for us?"

"You aren't thinking of using forbidden atomics?" Sandy said. There was little a Longknife could say that would shock a Santiago. Rita just had crossed that, among several other thresholds.

"The bug-eyed monsters have nukes," the elder woman said with finality. "They've thrown plenty of them at our ships and taken out a couple. They've also sent suicide nukes at Alwa. So far, we've only lost a few ships, but I'm thinking that if they're tossing them at us, it's only fair for us to have a few to toss back their way. It's been a nice three or four hundred years without them lurking in our closet, but sometimes you need to let some of your skeletons out to dance on someone's grave."

The room fell silent as they contemplated that goulash of mixed metaphors.

It was a long time before Ben started the conversation up again.

"Kris Longknife, and about all of us who have seen that crazy alien woman, heard her ravings and seen the horrors under their pyramid, have sworn that no new planets will be added to that house of horror. We feel honor bound to protect the cats."

He paused for a moment. "I also think the cats might be a good addition to our defense. As a race, they're pretty advanced. I could use a couple thousand of them working in my yards and manning the extra ships I build, along with regular Navy, Pipra's workers, Granny Rita's Colonials, and the birds of many feathers. I appreciate all the ships and gear that King Ray's alliance is sending out here, but we're the ones that will live or die at the bleeding point of this spear. With the cats, I think we have a better chance of living, and I *know* the cats have a better chance with a fleet of our ships in their sky."

That, in so many ways, let the cat out of the bag.

Sandy leaned back in her chair, eyed the overhead and tried to catch up with all the wild twists and turns of this conversation. She'd brought the *Victory* into the yard for some of that crystal armor and some serious maintenance. She'd figured she would have a little time to read a stack of reports and get up to speed on her new assignment.

When these three first walked in, she figured she had Ben and Pipra's needs pretty clear and wondered what this dottering old woman was doing here.

Big mistake.

Sandy reviewed the bidding and chose a different tack.

"Pipra, how is that problem you had when we last met? How are those managers that Alex Longknife sent out here to stripmine those streams for unique plants?"

"No problem," Rita said. "With only a little help from my great-granddaughter, Kris Longknife, I bounced their asses so high that the ship they had passage out of here on had to catch them on the way down. They, and a few other of my wayward son Al's ilk, were told they were *persona non gratis* in the Alwa system and were lucky to have passage back. Otherwise, I'd put them to work as farm labor, about the only real work they were good for."

"And you did this by what authority?" Sandy asked. She was, if she remembered correctly, the only Grand Admiral in the room.

"By my authority as Granny Rita, and if you insist, Viceroy."

Sandy got real soft with her next words. "King Raymond appointed me Viceroy to stand in his stead to the Alwa people."

"No doubt he appointed you, but did he show you the fine print on his contract with the Alwa Colonials?" the gray-haired woman asked so sweetly.

Sandy had been shown no fine print. She'd taken the King at his word that the big print was all that mattered to him. *Damn you, Longknifes!*

When Sandy said nothing, Granny Rita went on. "Kris Longknife was Viceroy only to the Colonials, and that, only if they voted her as such. To the birds, she was at best, an ambassador. More like a consular officer to stamp visas. As powerful and powerless as anyone in the flock of flocks."

Sandy tried to ignore the word blizzard and pick out the one snowflake in the storm. "The Colonials elected her Viceroy?"

"Yep. Took a vote. Folks were in an unusually generous mood. They figured it for a wedding gift to Kris, seeing that they were eating her wedding cake and all."

"Tricky thing, that," Admiral Benson put in.

"You wouldn't believe how independent these people are down there," Pipra added. "Likely comes from staying alive with only their own two hands to keep them that way."

"Wedding gift?" Sandy echoed.

"Yep," Rita answered.

"And you say I'm going to need to be voted into the Viceroy job?"

"Yep."

Sandy made a face. "Can't think of anyone I'd really like to marry today."

"So, have I got a deal for you," Rita said, gleefully. "You be the appointed Viceroy here topside, and I'll be the

Viceroy dirtside. I won't have any problem being voted in. Everything will be just fine. We'll work together to get everything done just jake," the old woman finished, her hand, once again, was held out to be shaken.

Sandy leaned well back in her chair and kept her hands on its arms.

Rita took her hand back.

It took Sandy a moment to reopen the conversation. "You may recall, Rita, that Santiagos who get too close to one of those damn Longknifes tend to end up dead. You can use any name you want, but right now, a Longknife is what I see sitting across from me. Not wanting to end up dead, I think we need to talk before we shake hands or sign agreements or cut our thumbs for a blood oath. What do you say?"

Rita settled back in her chair. "Seems reasonable."

"And, I may need some time before I can get myself to trust you."

"If Ray was my only idea of a Longknife, I'd likely agree with you."

"Pipra, how's production going?" Sandy said, changing direction.

"Fine. The folks we pulled off of the battlecruisers that came in here bent up and limping have pitched in with the hands that stayed moonside. We've got the fabs humming again. Now that the story is out that we've again kicked some serious alien butt out of Alwa's sky, we're getting more Roosters and Ostriches wandering in from the forests and savannas to ask for jobs that can get them those nice toys they like. I'm using the new recruits on consumer goods and promoting the experienced hands to heavy industry. I won't bore you with the industrial production goals we're aiming for, but they're pretty much what Kris Longknife worked out before she headed off to kill aliens. Plenty for the Navy, plenty for the Colonials and Alwans, and some left over so I can grow my base. I've already got the three new factories that you brought out settled down near the moon's north polar region. Right now, I've got them working on building a new heavy industry fab," Granny Rita began to cloud up. Pipra hurried on, "and two more light fabs for consumer products. By the way, you brought out a station and yard ship. We haven't needed it yet, so we didn't deploy it pending developments."

"Could it be the start of a base above Susquan?" Ben asked.

"Putting a base out there is not something anyone is going to stampede me into," Sandy said. "And I'm not going to visit those cats until I feel Alwa is safe."

"I heard tell there were some that got away from the last dust up?" Granny Rita asked.

Sandy scowled. "We got about a third of them, but the others broke up into small groups and hit the jump out of there at different speeds. I imagine they then broke up into smaller groups. Anyway, by the time we took care of the ambush they set up at one jump, the others were long gone, so we headed back."

"And got here too late to hold the baby. Oh, my, Ruthie is a darling."

"I've held a few babies in my time," Sandy answered, dryly, and again changed the subject. "Ben, how's the base force and yard work going?"

"While you were gone, we managed to up-armor all forty-eight of the ships you brought out. As you may have noticed, we were ready and waiting for you. I've run thirty-two of the less damaged battlecruisers through the yards and they're now shipshape and Bristol fashion. I've held off on the more damaged ships until Admiral Kitano got back so we can see which of her ships should be run through quickly ahead of them.

"The beam ships are a world of hurt unto themselves. I got all three of them moored together trailing the station by a hundred klicks. Kris Longknife had a repair ship tied up to each one of them before the fight and I've added a second. Between the two, they're doing what they can. There's no way we can get any of those monsters into a yard. We'll have to refit them where they lay. As of the latest report, one of them is busted up beyond all hope of repair. The second one might be able to get one beam working if we gave them a week's notice. The last one has two beams working. If we cannibalized the first ship, we might get that one full up to speed. Then again, I hear that all three were built at different planets and no one paid all that much attention to specs and standards. The folks working on them say they're more of a work of art than a manufactured product."

Sandy had heard something along that line when she was back in human space; this came as no surprise. More were in the pipeline. Hopefully, they'd be built more to a single standard than these three.

"Did a report on how the beam ships stood up to the pressures of a fight go back with Kris Longknife?" Sandy asked.

"Full analysis on the failure points of each of the ships."

"Good."

Benson went on to conclude with, "As I see it, we've got ninety-six battlecruisers ready to answer bells. You just brought in another eighty-eight. Some of those will need yard time, like your *Victory*. For the rest, ma'am, things are getting mighty crowded along the piers."

Sandy saw where this was going. "So I either take some

of those ships out for a visit to the cats or we have to break out *Kiel Station* and use it here, at least for a while."

"Pretty much, ma'am." Admiral Benson answered.

Sandy leaned back in her chair again. She seemed to be doing that a lot.

"So, you bunch of thieves want me to leave the hen house all to yourselves while I go gallivanting out to see if the cats can be tamed."

"Don't you know, Admiral," Pipra said through a huge grin, "cats can't be tamed."

"Yeah, right. Okay," Sandy said, and tapped her comm-link. "Get me Kitano."

"Yes, Admiral."

"I want a full briefing in my flag plot at 0900 hours tomorrow on the defensive situation around the Alwa System. Absent any threats, risks, or surprises, I'm looking to take one fleet out for a 'show the flag' to Sasquan. I'll want your recommendations on that idea tomorrow as well as who might be the best admiral and which ships are in the best shape to go."

"Aye, aye, ma'am. Pardon me for asking, but have those three rascals gotten to you?"

"Three rascals?"

"I heard Granny Rita, Ben, and Pipra were headed your way."

"Yep, they got to me."

"Tell them I want to see them at the briefing then. Kris did a pretty good job of keeping me in the loop where that bunch of troublemakers were concerned."

"I'll have them there. Santiago out."

Sandy leaned forward in her chair, resting her elbows on her desk. "Do I need a guard dog to guard my guard dogs?"

"Nobody here but us barkers and biters," Granny Rita said through a grin that clearly had too much cream in it.

Suspecting she'd regret this, she extended her hand. Rita took it and they shook.

"See you at 0900," Sandy said and the three filed out.

11

Two weeks later, Grand Admiral Sandy Santiago stood at the elbow of Vice Admiral Drago as his *Relentless* led his reinforced 4th Fleet into orbit around Sasquan. Trailing them was *Kiel Station* that might or might not be permanently deployed there. The success of her negotiations with the cats would determine that.

Still, with forty battlecruisers, it was better to have the station available, even if it proved temporary.

Surrounding Sandy on her shared flag bridge was a number of people the cats would find familiar.

The sociologist Jacques laDuke and his wife, Amanda Kutter, an economist, had taken time away from the many duties they'd taken on in the Colonial government of Alwa to come with Sandy back to Sasquan. Actually, they'd both jumped for the chance to see how things were going with the felines. Sandy couldn't have kept them away with a club.

She'd also brought Captain Penny Pasley with her. Penny and Commander Masao were Sandy's two top experts on the bug-eyed aliens, Penny having lead the scout sweep that found the alien's home world. Sandy was none too sure she'd need Penny's expertise on this trip, but Penny was also associated with one of Nelly's children, Mimzy, and Sandy wanted to get to know one of them.

Considering the warlike reputation of the cats, Sandy had also brought along General Steve Bruce to command her ships' Marines in case she had to launch a ground force. He, like Penny, had one of Nelly's kids that he'd named Chesty.

Out of the corner of her eye, Sandy eyed her newly minted captain. Penny seemed to be a bit uncomfortable with her new rank. Or maybe she was just uncomfortable around Sandy.

Sandy still remembered when her destroyer, *Halsey,* had come alongside a tumbling bit of wreckage and her crewmen had pried the beat up and bleeding living people from Kris Longknife's fast attack boat.

Kris and Penny had been among the living.

Tommy, Penny's husband of just a few days, was among the dead.

His family had come a quarter of the way across the galaxy from Santa Maria to attend the wedding only a few days earlier. A few days later, they were grouped around a sealed coffin. The Navy had done the best they could to keep it out of the news, but the media had gotten wind of it because a Longknife was involved. The service had turned into a real media circus.

Sandy had attended because it was her ship's crew that had recovered the body . . . and because she was a Santiago and Kris was starting to look like a Longknife. Sandy had insisted that sailors from the *Halsey* provide the honor guard, fire the salute, and bring everyone to cathartic tears with a properly played 'Taps.' The *Halsey's* XO offered the flag to the grieving widow. Penny had stood, or tried to stand to attention, half-supported by her former commanding officer, Kris Longknife.

Sandy had been studying the two, so she couldn't help but notice the grief-stricken look that swept over both of them at that moment.

Sandy had to turn away from the raw emotions fleeing across those two women's faces. Still, she was left with a question she'd never answer. Who was grieving most? The woman who married Tommy or the woman who hadn't?

Grand Admiral Santiago shook herself out of the past and back to the present. She turned to Admiral Drago. "How long is that list of people who want to talk to me?"

"Three feet tall and growing, ma'am," he said with a grin that would have suited a pirate of old. He'd admitted to Sandy on the voyage out that he was half-tempted to rename the *Relentless* the *Golden Hind* after Drake's flag ship. He was a pirate after the admiral's own heart who had circumnavigated the Earth in the long ago age of exploration because the Spanish had half a fleet out intent on hanging him for stealing their silver and gold.

"Certainly, none of the people we'll be dealing with, most especially not those soul-less, bug-eyed monsters, would get any of the extra meaning in the name."

"And how did Kris Longknife take to your idea?"

The pirate scowled. "The woman has no sense of humor or of history. At least not since she got her third stripe. Certainly not since she made admiral."

"So it's *Relentless*."

"*Relentless* as ever."

Once again, Sandy had to drag her mind back to the business at hand. At least this time it was from the less distant past. "So, everyone wants part of my time. How considerate of them. Who is actually going to see me this visit?"

Sandy turned away from the main screen filled with the images of ships doing what they knew very well how to do, thank you very much. Sandy had done the proper admiral thing and ordered Kiel Station to stand by to spin itself out, deploy its piers, and take on enough spin to provide the 'feel' of gravity. Neither Sandy nor anyone else was aware of a time when a station like the Kiel had been ordered to close itself up, suck in its piers, regenerate some rocket motors, and get underway again.

There's always a first time. Of course, Alwa Station would lead the way.

While they still had gravity, Sandy lead her team into the day cabin she shared with Admiral Drago. Before they'd deployed on this cruise, the *Relentless* had been pumped full of another five thousand tons of Smart Metal™ so that it could function as a flagship and support the expanded staff Sandy required. She'd balked at a few things, such as the installation of a Forward Lounge like the one Kris Longknife always seemed to have on her ships.

Even without alcohol, she didn't doubt that Admiral Drago was allowing his crew the freedom of Alwa Station's new Fraternization Policy.

"Do you have a woman aboard?" Sandy had asked her new admiral herself.

"My wife is a Colonial gal," he explained. "She figures if God had intended people to travel through space, He would not have given us this addiction to oxygen. So, no. My night quarters are my own."

They'd chosen to share a Flag plot and bridge, and a single spacious day office, though if matters got loud, they could raise a wall between their desks and do as they pleased.

They had separate night quarters off the day quarters.

Seated around a conference table, with their lap belts dogged down, if not snugged in tight, Sandy posed a question to her team. "How have matters changed since you were last here?"

With a nod from the others, Penny took over the briefing. "We've been intercepting their radio and television transmissions since we jumped into the system. Ah, Admiral, when we first were spotted by the Sasquans the time we had to fight off an alien attack on them, Kris Longknife was barraged by messages from everyone; governments, celebrities, advertisers, you name it. She chose to only talk to two kids, Zeth and Frodir. I've been in touch with them. They're both space-bitten and about to jump out of their hides to have us back.

"Their attitude is pretty much an echo, if a bit tinged with childish enthusiasm, for the rest with one exception."

Penny paused to clear her throat. "The feline populations fall into four national or rather super-national groups. The Bizalt Kingdom and Columm Almar are two major power blocks that basically dominate the world at this point. Both appear to have a functioning democracy, although we keep getting reports that sometimes legislative issues are resolved by duels. We can't quite figure out if that is a metaphor or a fact from what we understand of the media reporting. There is a third block, formally ruled rather brutally by a cat named Solzen. She, oh, Admiral, all the players here are female, anyway, she made the mistake of firing rockets at us last visit and Kris flattened her hideaway. That power block is now broken up among several squabbling warlords who don't seem to live very long and whose borders are very fluid.

"Finally, there is a group that call themselves unaligned. They refuse to be part of either of the three main alliances, although recent history shows that they aren't against joining one side or the other to restore the balance of power. That, a balance of power, appears to be the best peace these folks could hope for. At least before we showed up."

"And now?"

Jacques took over the briefing. "Kris challenged them to a race for their moon. But she insisted that they all had to win it together or she'd declare them all the loser."

Sandy ran a hand through her hair as it began to float away. The *Relentless* was now in free fall. "So, they throw a wad of money into technical research. It does all kinds of things to boast their economy while, at the same time, they discover they share the universe with not one, but two alien life forms, one of which wants them dead. How's that working?"

Jacques glanced at his wife. She took over.

"Pretty much like you'd expect. They're spending money on education and research. They're developing new techs and putting people to work. They've had a booming economy since the day we broke orbit. The unaligned countries approached this cautiously, but they got some of the contracts for the moon program and it brought them into the team."

"Is there enough to go around?"

"Admiral," Penny put in, "they aren't just aiming to put a cat on the moon and bring her back safely. They intend to establish a space station and a base on the moon, then send some ships to that outer planet where an alien hulk is rolling in orbit. I'm afraid that if we don't bring them into our orbit, they're going to come shooting into it, and I'm not sure we'd like them that way."

"So you're telling me we better assimilate them now, gently, or they will join us later, maybe not so gently."

"You could always leave a trail of breadcrumbs and get some wandering alien wolf pack to wipe them out," Drago said, darkly.

"You know that's not an option," Sandy said, glowering at her junior admiral.

"Yes, I know it, and you know it, and we need to keep that in mind as we find our way gingerly through this mine field."

"Yeah," Sandy said, and sighed.

Did I used to sigh so much, before I got stuck filling Kris Longknife's shoes? Damn, did she find this kind of stuff easier?

Mentally, Sandy shook her head. No one found this sort of stuff easy.

"Okay, where do we go from here?"

"You've been invited to meet with their Associated Peoples. It's kind of a meeting place for all their countries to get together and talk. Talk only. No action. Did I mention that they don't have a central government?" Penny asked.

"It's only in all the reports," Sandy said dryly.

"The first time we hacked into the TV net that showed the debate on the floor of their Associated Peoples' great hall," Penny said, "most of the talk sounded like verbal battles. We've been tracking their talking points since we arrived. They're more concerned with technological transfer and who gets what contracts. I hope all first contacts go as smoothly as this one."

"Those cats have nuclear triggers under their furry claws," Admiral Drago pointed out. "This job ain't over until it's over and done with. Don't any of us forget that."

"Amen," Sandy said, heartily, then smiled at Penny, lest she feel ganged up on by her bosses.

"I won't," the young woman assured her.

Out on her bridge, one of her sailors lost his lunch, explosively. Sandy's scowl this time was for mother nature and her failure to design the human body for space.

"Admiral, pass the word to *Kiel Station*. Based on Captain Pasley's briefing, I have determined that it is more likely than not that we will make Kiel Station a permanent fixture in the felines' sky. Spin her out, and if need be, anchor the ships nose-to-nose until she's ready to dock us."

"Aye, aye, ma'am," Admiral Drago said, and quickly began muttering into his commlink.

12

Sandy's actual introduction to the felines was one surprise after another. Her admiral's barge set down smoothly in the harbor of a bustling city whose name was unpronounceable but Penny's Mimzy was calling New York for some reason. What Sandy saw from the barge's windows was a city of high rises and skyscrapers with wide expanses of windows gleaming silver in the noon day sun.

This could be Wardhaven.

Two longboats full of Marines had been deployed ahead of her and a pair of armed longboats had followed her down with more Marines.

"Did you notice in the reports you read, Admiral," Penny had explained when Sandy asked why all the fuss, "that someone took a shot at Kris? We think she was from that crazy bunch that shot at us and we flattened, but we never heard back from the cats as to whether or not they got to the bottom of it. We're not taking any chances this time out."

"So, I'm as much of a target as Kris Longknife."

"Yes, Admiral, that's why we had spidersilk under-armor

laid out for you this morning," Penny said, and tugged at the neck of the transparent body suit she wore.

"You think I've got a target painted on my backside?"

"I very much doubt it, ma'am, but I'm not paid to let the people around me get suddenly dead. I've connected with the police that I knew from our last visit. They are on their highest alert level. Right now, in town, they've got all their world's heads of state, chiefs of state, and other dignitaries, not to mention most of the women of finance and industry. They don't want any old grudges being settled on their watch. They definitely don't want you so much as scratched. They're on it, ma'am. Those Marines are just for show, not that General Bruce doesn't have them kitted out for anything and everything. You've got the same full, all-around detail that Kris Longknife traveled with, science and high tech to prevent the shot, and forensic to clean up the mess if someone gets one off."

"I can't tell you how glad I am," Sandy said, dryly.

"Neither was Kris, but this team kept her alive against more shots than any common human being had any right to survive."

"Kris Longknife is certainly not a common human being," Sandy said.

"Amen," answered Penny.

After the admiral's barge motored ashore, Sandy was greeted by both the feline that ran the city and the one that ran the district, which seemed to have the same name as the city. Penny stayed at Sandy's side, Mimzy at her collarbone, translating the conversation both ways. It seemed to go well and deviated not one whit from what Sandy would have enjoyed from any human city excited to be celebrating Fleet Week.

They'd laid on a major parade, for which Sandy found

herself riding in a bubble atop some sort of float. She did notice, as she climbed into the bubble that the glass looked to be two inches thick and the float rode on sixteen thick tires in eight pairs.

"You think they're going out of their way to protect me?" Sandy asked Penny.

"The transport is a relic of when wars were plentiful and political assassinations were a thing of policy," Mimzy answered. "They hauled it out of a museum when we jumped into the system, replaced the bulletproof glass, and checked it out thoroughly. I was told that the police don't expect anything untoward, but they are taking no chances."

"Oh, and they put it out in the news that having you ride in this is a great honor, not a precaution at all," Mimzy added.

"You think anyone believes that?" Sandy asked.

"Not one word of it," Penny answered, "but, for what it's worth, neither their police nor their intelligence agencies, and that's both the Royal and Columm Almar working together, have any hint of trouble."

"I can't tell you what a relief that is to my worried mind," Sandy said.

"That's sarcasm, right?" Mimzy said.

"Yes, dear," Penny answered. "You aren't meant to believe what she just said."

"Humans. Mother was right."

"Mother being Nelly?"

"Yes, Admiral. They really are a family."

Sandy took a few minutes to wave and smile at a crowd that seemed to be six deep on the sidewalks, eager to wave at her, but not pushing either the police or uniformed riot troopers that stood with their back to Sandy and face to the crowd.

"You like having Mimzy at your neck?"

"Yes, ma'am, though it is an education. One that runs both ways. I couldn't help but notice that all you have is a rather old commlink on your wrist."

"It's met all my needs."

"You might find it helpful to be on Nelly Net, as the kids call it. It's almost like telepathy between us. For example, General Bruce just alerted me that a scuffle broke out two blocks ahead. His drones are keeping an eye on it, but it hasn't shown up on radio so we don't have any news about it."

"Do you think it's strange that it's not on the radio net? They do know we're monitoring it."

"Yes, Admiral. I am a bit concerned, but both Steve and I know that the cats are quite intent on keeping a perfectly nice face turned in our direction."

"I can't blame them for the effort, but it does leave me wondering if there is another face out there. What are we meant not to see?" Sandy asked.

"That is hard to tell, ma'am. I can understand their attitude. I'd do the same if I was in their shoes. Still, I'm in my own shoes and I'm not at all sure what I'm dealing with. Oh, and I can never forget for one moment that the society we're dealing with has a nuclear button. Yep. Concerned today. That's me."

The drive from the landing pier to the skyscraper that held the headquarters of the Associated Peoples passed with no unscheduled activities. The fancy rig was too tall to make it into the garage, so Sandy entered through the front door under a huge portico. She couldn't help but notice that the portico was hung with festive bunting and streamers that flowed from the top to almost ground level.

Sandy winced softly. No sniper was going to get a good

shot at her from the nearest building. For a people doing their best to put their best paw forward, these cats looked awful antsy.

Kris Longknife had addressed the Universal Assembly, to great applause. Sandy found herself being hurried through the marble halls to an elevator and whisked up to the top of the tower. There she was ushered into one huge room that would have given her agoraphobia if she was susceptible to that fear after thirty-seven years in the Navy, and half of it spent in space.

Under a clear, arching ceiling, the entire floor was a single expanse of tan, pebbled marble. Here and there, the vastness was broken by potted plants or trees. In some cases, the vegetation formed shaded paths to granite outcrops with softly flowing waterfalls. The sun streamed in, dazzling the scene as it would any equatorial ecosystem.

Sandy was suddenly swept with the impression that she had stumbled into some vast, arid plain. Even as she was greeted warmly by two large cats, a primal urgency rose in her belly, fight or flight. It took a serious effort by Sandy not to feel where her service automatic rode in the small of her back.

With a deep sigh, she stepped out of the elevator, extended her hand, and prepared to meet, human to cat.

A long line stretched away from the elevator, but at the head of the line were the two she'd expected to see. President Almar of Columm Almar stood first. She wore a violet coat with silver trim and buttons today. Like all the cats present, that was all she wore; the fact that she was female was not in doubt.

She extended her own paw, claws retracted respectfully, and presented a smile full of teeth and twitching whiskers. "I am happy to greet you in the name of the Congress of

Columm, in the name of our people, and on my own behalf. May I say that I am so glad that you humans have survived your war and chosen to return to us. I can't help but note that you have come back with more warships this time, and even something that looks suspiciously like a space station, or so I am told."

"Yes, I have my 4th Fleet for an escort this visit," Sandy said smoothly and Mimzy translated from Penny's neck. "With so many ships, it seemed a good idea to bring a space station. Kiel Station may become a permanent star in your sky, or we could have it follow us out just as it followed us in."

"No doubt, we will enjoy discussing that with you."

"Al, don't hog the woman so. Hello, it is my honor to greet you in the name of the ancient parliament of the Bizalt Kingdom and in the name of our monarch and the people of our ancient land, as well as myself. I must admit that I find your space station idea very interesting. As you may have heard from our media, we are intent on orbiting a station of our own, though a much smaller one, no doubt.

"Gerrot, don't twaddle," interrupted President Almar. "Tell us. Who are you and what authority do you bring? We know you are at war with an abomination. How can a small and backward people like us expect but to be used in your fight?"

"Al," Madame Gerrot interrupted the interruption, and swatted at the other leader for emphasis. "Didn't your mother teach you to share your food? Let the poor woman at least introduce herself before you decide if she is pride or prey."

"You saw that young one that was here last," Al grumbled. "They are certainly not prey."

"Then treat her with the respect you'd treat a victorious warrior."

The debate between the two leaders paused for a moment, and Sandy took the initiative.

"Please allow me to introduce myself. I am Grand Admiral Maria Santiago," Sandy said, choosing to pretty much go with Kris Longknife's introduction. "I am commissioned Viceroy to the people of Alwa and Command the Alwa Defense Sector. I am enjoined by my King to greet you in the name of the people of the United Society, their congress and my liege, King Raymond, the First of that name. And, as Kris Longknife said before me, I stand before you in peace and greet you in the name of all humanity as well as the Iteeche Empire, may we long share peace with them, and the people of Alwa. May I add, that in the time that has passed, and that you appear to have put to very good use, the Alwa Defense Sector has grown while destroying six alien raider wolf packs and likely killed a trillion individual aliens."

There had been a low murmur in the room as those waiting to talk to Sandy quietly shared their thoughts with each other. They had fallen to a whisper as she introduced herself.

The vast room was swept by a wave of deadly silence at Sandy's final words.

"A trillion," Madame Gerrot whispered into it as if careful not to disturb the dead. "That many?"

"Their mother ships are gigantic," Sandy pointed out, "easily the size of small moons. Their warships are huge and many, and growing more plentiful even as we slaughtered them in the hundreds and by the thousands."

The President of Almar shivered inside her violet jacket.

"I had thought that some of our ancestors were hard and bitten warriors. You humans . . ." she gave up her search for words.

Sandy would have given half her pension to console the cats, but consolation was not her mission here. "We are no harder than we must be to defeat the foe that goes for our throats. However, let us ignore them for the moment. Their handful of desperate survivors that managed to flee far from our pursuers have crawled away to lick their wounds and seek succor from those of their own kind that they would normally avoid. We are victorious and we now must look to our future and the forming of alliances."

Sandy raised her voice to carry as far as the vast room would allow. "Word of you has reached the ear of my King. He has received one of your own into his presence and they have discussed how your needs and ours might be in harmony. I am charged and required by King Raymond to, when time and opportunity allow, meet with you and see what we can do to further our mutual advantages."

That brought applause to the room.

It had only just begun to die down when President Almar took a short step toward Sandy. "What mutual advantages might your King be willing to grant to a people who are so far behind you technologically and scientifically that we must seem little better than animals to you?"

The Prime Minister of the Bizalt Kingdom was right at the president's sleeve. "We know what it is like for the weaker to enter into an agreement with the stronger. We do not like the taste of that meat. Not at all, not at all."

"Then we must talk more on it, mustn't we?" Sandy said.

Both sighed. "But for now, let us introduce you to more people than you will ever remember, and let them tell you of what their country is doing in this all-for-one race to the moon. When we are done, we may have something for you to see."

"Something?"

"No one will be aboard it, but we think we are ready to touch our moon with a rock we tossed ourselves," the prime minister said, slyly.

This was not a surprise for Sandy. The sensor team had identified the media excitement over the upcoming moon launch. The objective was simple: land a probe on their moon, softly if possible, but any landing would do.

The alien's space programs both in the last year and before their contact with humans, had shown many fiery failures.

Sandy, with Penny and her Mimzy, moved down the receiving line, shaking paws with each president or prime minister, or, in a few instances, a monarch. A translator had appeared at Penny's elbow; she did the introductions, leaving Mimzy to translate the few words that passed between them. Most had a particular part of the rocket they were working on, either developing or building this rocket or the bigger ones to come. Several of them were quick to mention that they had ceased their border war with this or that state and submitted it to the International Tribunal.

"Mimzy?" Sandy asked the third time someone preened at the fact they were settling their problem by measures other than war.

"The International Tribunal was a moribund body the last time we visited. It seems to have taken on quite a workload since," the computer answered.

"Interesting," Sandy said, and moved on to the next cat.

The two major leaders were right; Sandy shook the hand

of more cats than she could ever possibly remember. Still, they saw her, and she saw them. They got to show their pride in what they were doing, be it scientific, industrial, or just not killing each other.

So far, it was an interesting visit.

13

A long hour later, Sandy found herself with the president and prime minister back at her elbow, guiding her and Penny toward a corner of the great room. As they approached, Sandy found herself looking at something right out of a grassy plain. It was decked out like a sylvan glen, complete with gently flowing waterfall and shady trees. In the middle of the created green space, with the trees to her right and to her left a wondrous view of city, sea, and sky, stood a long, thick, wooden table with chairs around it for ten.

Sandy had a recollection from somewhere that animals in the wild maintained some sort of truce of the water hole. Everyone needed to drink, so even the most hungry carnivore did not stalk prey around the one place they could get water. The admiral wondered if this place had been arranged as some sort of subliminal recreation of that primal truce.

Seven cats were already seated around the table in comfortable tall chairs which had openings at the bottom of the backs for tails. These were already swishing: some furiously, some lazily, but all showing something to those around them.

Too bad I don't have a tail.

Sandy was led to the chair at the head of the table; President Almar and Madame Gerrot waited while she seated herself, with Penny standing at her right elbow. The two then took the chairs beside her, sweeping their tails gracefully behind them and into the hole in the chair provided.

Several cats wearing leather harnesses of red, blue, green, and yellow appeared out of the woods to stand right behind about half of the participants, including the two most powerful, the president and the prime minister.

"We, like you, have our own translators," President Almar said. "We will accept the translation of your device as the official translation unless we think there is a problem with our understanding of your words."

Sandy nodded, reminded once again that words were slippery things at best. When words tried to cross cultures, much less species, matters could be as crazy as chasing greased pigs. Again, she found herself wishing she was at least on that mental net that Nelly's humans seemed to share.

Next trip down, I'll be better prepared.

"So," Madame Gerrot said, "what can we poor creatures do for you?"

Sandy did not like the sound of that. "First, let me clear the atmosphere. No one who has mastered the use of nuclear weapons strikes me and my people as 'poor creatures.' You are very capable and it appears that you have, since being introduced to the harsh reality that you are not alone in the galaxy, concentrated your minds and your efforts very admirably."

"As you can understand, the discovery that some alien

life form could snuff us all out like we might stomp a colony of ants was most disturbing and served to concentrate our thoughts," Madame Gerrot replied.

"I am curious," President Almar said. "When Kris Longknife first visited, she seemed to view us as a distraction. Are we still a distraction?"

Sandy turned to Penny and raised an eyebrow. *You go, girl.*

"You must remember that when Kris Longknife discovered you, she was in hot pursuit of a group of mutineers who had stolen a starship. Finding you was more of a surprise than a distraction. Then the surprise was compounded by finding a primitive alien monster base where those we had defeated were licking their wounds and plotting further attacks on us or you. In order to defend you from annihilation, we had to make contact, a contact we were not at all prepared to follow through with. As Admiral Kris Longknife told you, we knew that Alwa was about to come under attack. As it turned out, we were attacked by even more aliens than we expected. So, please let me ease any false assumptions you may have acquired during Kris Longknife's first visit. Then we were taken by surprise and unprepared for a proper mission. As Admiral Santiago has told you, this is an entirely new initiative intent on peaceful contact and the establishment of mutually beneficial relations."

Those around the table seemed to mull that over for a long moment. As they did, Sandy eyed the table. It was a good forty centimeters thick, not the thing you threw around. However, its surface showed deep gashes, some repaired with putty, others just sanded over. Apparently, these kitties had claws and they could come out if things got intense.

Wonder how the spidersilks would do in a claw fight?

A cat from down the table spoke next. She wore a transparent golden cape that shimmered alluringly. "So, what are your intentions now? What do you want from us?"

Sandy was ready for that.

"I came to see how you were doing. I also brought the ships that I could spare with the hopes that you might want us to establish a permanent presence in your system."

"Are these enough ships to defend us from a serious attack?" the President of Columm Almar asked sharply.

"No, my 4th Fleet could not repulse an attack from a full wolf pack."

"Then what good would it be in our sky?" the golden cape demanded.

"Around Alwa, we have established an automated picket system, outposts covering star systems many jumps out from Alwa. This gives us warning of developing threats. With warning, we can call for reinforcements or conduct spoiling attacks that delay the alien's main thrust. Are you familiar with such tactics in your history?"

"Yes, we know of this way of waging war. You would do this for us?" Madame Gerrot asked.

"That is a proposal that I am ready to lay on the table."

"That is a large and tasty kill that you have laid before us," the golden caped one said. "What would you want for such a thing, our first-born cub?"

Sandy could only look at the feline with curiosity, she then glanced at Penny. "Did something get lost in translation?"

Around the table, several primaries were suddenly in conversation with their translators. No doubt, Sandy's open aside to Penny had stoked any paranoia they'd brought to the table.

Mimzy said something in feline, then added in Standard, "I just told them what you asked of Penny. Now their translators are agreeing that what I told them is what you said. Now they are translating what I'm saying now. This could go on forever. Let me say something." And Mimzy dropped back into cat.

Sandy found herself sitting ignored as negotiations went on without her. She did not care for this, but she held her temper.

"Now," Mimzy said, speaking in cat out of one side of herself, and Standard out of the other, "our friends, the Sasquans, have many folk tales of warlocks that offer something of great worth in return for the warrior's first born. It is a tale of warning. We humans have similar tales, though we rarely make a reference to them during serious negotiations. Now, my Admiral would like to make you an offer."

"Based upon our present resources, we cannot defend a second system. The correlation of space that needs defending with respect to forces available to do it just does not add up. We could give you warning. We could snipe at them on approach, but we just don't have the forces to defend you if the alien raiders make a serious effort against Alwa and you at the same time. Do you understand me on this?"

Heads nodded sideways. Sandy blinked at them, waiting.

Madame Gerrot surveyed the table, then spoke for them all. "Yes, the situation you describe is one we are only too familiar with. Is the question before us one of how you may gain a greater force?"

"You are correct, Madame. We are making ships, but what we lack are crew. The Alwans are a low technology culture. Tool users, but not industrialized. You are highly industrialized. I would like to recruit a levy of your warriors to train on my warships. I would like to recruit a force of your workers to work side by side with my fabrication workers to build goods and the heavy fabrications that go into our warships. Rather than wait for you to come to us in space, I am asking you to send your best to work with us and I will give them a ticket to space."

Sandy had hoped that her words would be met with a cheer, or at least a "hell yes." Instead, all the tail wagging stopped ... stopped dead.

The golden caped leader leapt to her feet; her paws sprouted razor-sharp claws ten centimeters long that raked deep into the table's wood. "You would shackle our young and take them away to slavery in chains!" She roared.

Mimzy translated in a whisper.

Sandy locked eyes with the big cat. Her coat was a tawny brown with darker and lighter spots, perfect camouflage for prowling a savannah. Now both paws were on the table, claws fully extended. Slowly, she raked them across the table.

The others around the table froze in place. None of them looked at Sandy or the standing big cat.

They waited for what would come next.

Wearing her most stony face, and without breaking eye contact, Sandy slowly reached under her dress blues coat, around to where her service automatic rested in the small of her back. Slowly, she removed it, brought her hand around, then whipped the gun hand out and, with a large arc, slammed the automatic down on the table.

"The next time you pull your claws on me, I will kill you," she said, low and deadly. Beside her, Mimzy translated it with the same inflections.

For a moment longer, the two stayed locked in their

confrontation, then the two seated cats beside the standing one rose very slowly. They gently took her elbows and urged her back, away from the others.

With a terrifying shriek, the cat whipped around and charged into the woods beside the table. Sandy could hear roars and screeches, but Mimzy translated nothing. A small tree was ripped up by its roots and thrown into the rippling pond, sending a tall wave in all directions to overflow its banks.

"Clearly, the meaning of my words was lost in translation," Sandy said. She spoke softly, and removed her hand from her automatic. She did not, however, remove it from the table.

"Yes, most definitely," Madame Gerrot said, "we must take another try at conveying to each other what you intended and what we heard."

Sandy noted that the raging temper was quieting down; she knew she should go on, but she felt compelled to recross that dangerous ground. "What did she hear?"

Most of the cats were still intent on studying the grain of the table's wood. None had their paws visible or looked Sandy's way . . . or at each other. Madam Gerrot attempted to fill the deadly silence, although even she would not look Sandy in the eye.

"In olden days, not so long ago for some, a victor might demand slave labor from the defeated, and carry many of the young off never to return. Some of us are most sensitive to that part of our history than others."

Sandy nodded. "In our old times, we did things like that as well, which we now find reprehensible. I would never demand something like that, even from a defeated enemy. Yet, I do not meet with you as a defeated enemy. I see you as an equal and wish to negotiate with you as such."

There was a pause as several of the cats risked eye contact with each other. Finally, Madame Gerrot attempted an answer.

"It is very hard for us to believe the words you say. Your Kris Longknife won a great victory. A victory that we contributed nothing to. In days of memory, the victor in a great battle would place demands nearly as harsh on those that did nothing to defend themselves as they did on those that fought against them. Do you understand?"

"I can understand that you have a history. What you must understand is that the battle was joined with Kris Longknife and the alien murderers long before she met you. Had she found them here, though your planet was as barren as your moon, she would have fought them."

Well, maybe not. Maybe Kris would have tiptoed away and then come back with a few more ships, but no need to make too fine a point here.

"The blood lust is that strong between you?" This time President Almar risked to raise his head.

"It is in our nature that, if we can, we will make peace with anyone who offers us the hand of peace. That is always the hand we choose first. These alien raiders refuse to offer us peace under any circumstances. The only offer that comes from their hand is death, so yes, death is what we give back to them. Death everywhere and in every way."

"And you ask us to join you in that fight to the death?" said President Almar.

"Yes, because it is your fight, as well. We face the same enemy and we face the same murder if we lose. In this, we are all equals. I ask you to let your people come to work with us so long as they wish to work for us. I promise them food, good shelter, and gifts that will make their work for us something they will tell their grandchildren about." Sandy prayed she'd gotten the list right this time. Those around the table seemed more than satisfied.

"Then let us agree to this, and let us show you what we have done with our own hands.

14

T he trip to the rocket launch was quite an experience.

Sandy had heard about maglev trains but she had never actually ridden in one. It felt very strange to be rushing at such high speeds over the verdant fields and through forests that went from something like human conifer and broadleaf to something very much like broadleaf palms while skirting tall jungle growth. Between going at some 400 kilometers per hour this close to the ground and the strange vegetation, it was well past weird.

They must have been very close to the equator when the train slowed and pulled into a station on the edge of a medium-sized city. While the station itself was empty except for a smattering of workers and a small legion of security and military types, the streets outside were thronged with cats.

They were not so much enthusiastic to see Sandy, as curious. The parade bubble transport had been shipped south, so once again Sandy and Penny found themselves riding through streets, looking down on crowded sidewalks full of curious people who just stared back. Only after a few smaller cats waved, and Sandy and Penny waved back, did the adult cats begin to show any excitement for the visit of these tailless strangers from the stars.

"Considering this city has to be deeply involved in their space program," Penny said, "I would have expected a lot more enthusiasm."

Sandy kept waving. "If you were a distant number two, you might be a bit more cautious toward the number one."

"You think that really bothers them?"

"I think that the cat in the golden cape was very para-noid about getting involved with us, and I think a lot of those around the table were not at all averse to her laying that out on the table, then staking it there with a long, sharp claw."

"Yeah," Penny agreed.

"So, where is General Bruce and how is our security going?"

"You've got two full platoons of Marines mixed in with this motorcade. He's at the cat's central security command post here in town. Everything is going just fine."

"And, besides that golden-caped leader, we're seeing no evidence that these cats are bothered by us walking among them?"

"Not even a whisper of evidence."

"Doesn't that bother you?"

"The short hairs on the back of my neck, Admiral, are doing a jig for some reason, but me, bothered? Never."

"Yeah, right."

They waved their way through town, then sped up on new roads that ran straight towards the distant coast. The foliage got lower as they drove onto sandier soil. Huge buildings slowly rose above the horizon directly ahead. One was likely a fabrication or construction building for the big rockets. Miles away, a tall, thin silver arrow was the cat peoples' hope for their future.

The cavalcade came to a stop several kilometers from the launch pad beside a low slung concrete bunker. A technical leader in a white coat led Sandy from her ride through a door with thick steel shutters and into a wide room where row upon row of technicians applied themselves to what looked like very primitive workstations. To her left was a long window which gave a perfect view of the launch pad. Frequently, the working cats would risk a glance up and eye their handiwork.

Sandy found herself eyeing it, too.

The rocket was now steaming off something.

"We will launch in less than, ah, fifteen of our minutes," Mimzy translated for Sandy.

"What are the chances that your rocket will blow up on the pad?" Sandy asked her tech handler.

She gave what Sandy was learning was a laugh, though it came out more as a hacked-off purr. "You may have seen some of the media footage of our failures."

"I was shown a mash up we took off your media of one explosion after another," Sandy admitted. "It seemed to have a laugh track attached."

"Yes, some people think our moon program is a joke. It doesn't help when our political overlords suddenly decide to throw money at a space administration that was making slow but sure progress. Suddenly, even the imperials are throwing money at the builders of rockets. So, we build rockets and push them out here for launching when they still need to spend more time on the test firing stands. Disgusting."

"What about this rocket?" Penny asked. "Is it too soon for it?"

The big cat nodded happily. "No. We have been over every millimeter of this rocket with our own claws. There will not be so much as a twitch when this one goes."

Sandy was taken to a line of seats in the back to watch the launch. It was crowded with other dignitaries, although Sandy noted the lack of major politicians.

Do they know something I don't?

As the launch moment approached, it became just like something out of an historical melodrama. The cats had even invented the countdown.

"Five. Four. Three. Ignition. Two. One. Zero . . . Liftoff!"

A few moments before the rocket took flight, the liquid fueled rocket motors had ignited, coughed, then steadied. At zero, four solid strap-on rocket engines lit off. They reached full power in less than a second and, with the liquid-fueled main engine, shot the rocket off the pad and straight into a perfectly azure sky without so much as a puff of a cloud in sight.

In a moment, there was nothing to see through the front windows but a huge, billowing cloud of white smoke.

Attention turned to several screens around the room. Many of them showed the rocket's progress from different tracking cameras. All of them were encouraging.

Sandy waited with growing need for a restroom break as the solid rockets peeled off like petals from a flower. When the main rocket fell silent, then fell away, the second stage rocket ignited and continued the journey heavenward.

"The second stage should power the moon rocket to orbit over the next five minutes and then fall away."

"It won't hit our space station and fleet, will it?" Penny asked. Sandy eyed her guide while she checked with another cat. "Your space station is well above where our probe will orbit. Also, one of your people gave us notice of a safe launch window that will allow us to reach the moon without going near your station."

"Very good," Sandy said. "Now, while that rocket is doing its thing, I find that I must do mine. Is there a restroom near at hand?"

That drew a blank stare.

"Toilet facility?" Penny offered.

Apparently, Mimzy's second guess was better than her first, and Sandy was pointed toward a door with a triangular sign on it. The one across from it had a straight line.

Interesting.

Sandy was half afraid that she'd find herself squatting over some sort of litter box, but she found stalls with toilets she could sit right down on. She closed the door, secured it in a rational manner, and settled to do her business.

As she contemplated her future with these kinds of creatures under her command, she heard a soft hissing sound. She glanced around to see if she could spot a leak, then recognized a smell. The odor wasn't offensive, nor was it anything she'd ever smelled before.

She started to stand, and found herself struggling to get her feet under herself. She reached for her automatic, but before she could draw it she found herself falling face forward onto the door.

Then she blacked out.

15

Captain Penelope Pasley, Chief of Alien Intelligence, which seemed to be covering more than one species at the moment, watched the rocket climb. Mimzy translated a lot of the chatter going on around the room. It sounded much like she would have heard from a human team who had just pulled off the Big One.

No one raised any alarms, but rather soft, confident voices continued a litany of all results being in the ball park.

The probe reached orbit. The second stage cut off and cut loose from the stage that would hurl it toward the moon and the final stage that would attempt a soft landing. Penny joined in the joy, exchanging well done's with many of the team that had done it and who were only too willing to include a human in their celebration.

Only when things quieted down did Penny notice a certain lack.

"Where's the toilet facilities?" she asked the cat she'd just been hugging.

She pointed Penny toward the back of the room and

down a corridor. Penny quickly climbed the steps to the viewing gallery above the top row of work stations and, catching sight of two rooms with markings, quickly headed in that direction.

Somewhere along the line, she picked up her minder.

"Is something wrong?"

"Where is the admiral?"

"Possible she stepped outside for a breath of air. Do you humans smoke soft medicates?"

"The admiral does not," Penny snapped. She reached the door and pushed it open.

One whiff of the smell told her she had trouble.

Stepping back, she let the door swing closed. "General Bruce, we may have a problem. I need a Marine in MOPP 4 gear and I needed him here yesterday."

"On his way," came from Mimzy.

The door to the front of the control center slammed open and a Marine dashed in, pulling his MOPP headgear shut and zipping it in place. He took the steps three at a time, scattering cats out of his way. Maybe he wasn't the one scaring the cats. Four Marines with weapons drawn trailed only a few steps behind him.

He got to Penny in hardly a moment.

"The problem is in here. A strange smell. The admiral was last reported in here."

"Aye, aye, ma'am," the Marine said, and pushed Penny gently aside. The Navy captain gave way, and the Marine entered the room and quickly closed the door. From inside, Penny heard a blower being switched on.

As Penny listened to bathroom stall doors being slammed open, another Marine weaseled her way to the front, knelt, and slipped a device under the door. She scowled, either at the result or at the crashing noise as the

Marine inside kicked in a stall, but she quickly pulled a small container from the satchel at her side, attached it to the device she'd run under the door, and then squeezed it.

"Three. Two. One," she counted down. Whether the count was for what she'd just sprayed inside or for the Marine, who slammed the door open, it didn't matter.

"The admiral is not in here," the heavily protected Marine reported. In his gloved hands, he held up her wrist commlink and her automatic.

"General Bruce," Penny reported through Mimzy, "the admiral is gone. I assume she has been taken. We are full Code Red."

"Roger," Bruce answered, "We are full Code Red. Drago, I want two battalions of Marines down on my site, a full technical team, and all necessary support. I want them now."

"They will be dropping in fifteen minutes."

"You cats have no idea what kind of hurt you have just brought down upon your heads," Penny said, turning to her minder. That cat was not in sight.

"Marines, seal this site," she ordered. She had two platoons on hand. They would be enough.

16

Grand Admiral Sandy Santiago came back to consciousness to find herself being towed along on a small trolley through a tight, dimly lit, and leaking dirt tunnel.

She had lost her pants. Apparently, whoever had grabbed her from the bathroom stall had applied cat logic to her dress and absconded with her in a coat, but nothing lower down.

Her naked lady parts weren't the worst of Sandy's problems.

Her legs were taped together both above and below the knees, her hands were likewise taped across each other at the wrist and her elbows were held to her body by more tape. A wad of toilet paper with a strange taste had been shoved into her mouth, then taped over.

Someone cornered the market on tape.

Sandy tried to see where she was going, and got her head scratched by one long claw. Whoever was towing her on this cart had two or three long claws into her dress blues coat and at least one, maybe two more available to cut her throat if the need arose.

Sandy settled in, made herself comfortable for the moment, and did her best to make sure no such need arose.

I bet Penny and General Bruce are having a conniption fit by now.

Sandy did check to make absolutely sure her service automatic hadn't ended up anywhere on her body.

Nope, it has gone to where my pants and panties headed off for.

Refusing to take the counsel of her fears, or let the tight, damp quarters or the dank air spook her, Sandy lay still, took long slow breaths, and waited for the situation to change.

There was no doubt in her mind that Penny and General Bruce would make sure it did.

17

P enny set her Marines to tearing the place apart, not waiting for General Bruce's reinforcements to arrive. There was a rubber mat before the sink and mirrors. When it would not move, she had Marines rip it up with their bayonets.

Under it they found the trap door they were looking for. It opened into a duct with a ladder that led straight down. No sooner was it open, than a female Marine was dropping down it, two rungs at a time.

"There's a room down here. I've found the admiral's dress blues pants and shoes."

"Is the air breathable?" her sergeant demanded.

"I think so. I'm breathing it."

Penny did not wait for an answer, but went down the ladder, her legs outside it, her hands dropping her two, maybe three rungs at a time.

Hitting hard, Penny dropped and rolled, taking the place in with a hasty glance. It was a service room. What looked like a furnace stood in one corner, power converters in another. Four quick strides took Penny to the single door. It

opened inward with a click. It led into another dusty industrial area that led back upstairs to the main launch
command center.

Penny shook her head. No half-naked admiral had been
paraded through there. "There has to be another way out
of here."

Returning to the open duct, Penny called up it. "Sergeant, get your team down here. I want this room searched
with a fine-tooth comb."

In a moment, Marines filled both rooms, each with a
square assigned to them, each looking for how this locked
room had swallowed their admiral.

The breakthrough came in the outer room.

"Captain, you'll want to see this."

Penny was at the elbow of a Marine corporal. She shone
her flashlight along the side of a supply cabinet.

"Grease, ma'am. Someone greased the floor here."

"Move that thing," Penny ordered.

Three burly Marines soon had the cabinet moving.
Behind it, carved into a concrete wall, was a square close to a
meter across. Inside that, was a dirt hole. The light showed
darkness; the corporal intensified the beam. Light reached
deeper into the tunnel.

It showed a pile of dirt. The tunnel had caved in.

Penny needed both arms to keep Marines from scram-
bling into the hole, to start digging with their bare hands.

"General Bruce, we've found a dirt tunnel that is likely
how they got the admiral out of here. It's collapsed, whether
by intent or accident, I don't know. I need engineers. Mimzy,
this is for transmission to all the major powers on this
planet. 'Grand Admiral Santiago has been kidnapped out of
the command bunker where she was observing the launch
of your moon probe. I call on all of you for assistance to

assure her safe return. I need not tell you that failure in this effort will have dire consequences for our future relationship.'"

That lets the cat out of the bag, Penny thought, and did not suppress a bitter smile at the thought of what must be happening around this world in its halls of power.

18

Sandy smelled a change in the air before the light started to get normal. She sensed a steady, brighter light, before she was rolled into a small cavern, dirt on all sides, with rough wood for a roof and a muddy, clay floor.

Two cats in muddied fur, not wearing harnesses and without markings, pulled her up from the cart and stood her roughly on her feet.

"Does anyone speak Standard?" Sandy asked as she swayed unsteadily on her bare feet. She'd lost her shoes somewhere along the line. Standing tall proved to be both hard and painful as the tape pulled savagely on her skin as she forced it to stretch and let her stand.

"Talk, you, no," the muddied cat at her right elbow said.

There were four cats in the room. Two holding her, one who'd dragged her and was out of breath, and a single other, a male. His pelt was white where it wasn't filthy with mud. He was intently staring at some sort of instrument and ignoring the rest.

"Why am I here?" Sandy asked, trying for simple and direct.

That got her cuffed. No claws, but those paws packed a wallop. Sandy bounced off the one who could speak and ended up on the muddy floor.

The two pulled her back up to her feet.

The one that hit her and the one that dragged her exchanged growls while the possible translator steadied the admiral on her feet.

That's gonna leave a mark.

The male growled something and the other two stopped their argument. He said something more and got an answer from the potential translator. They talked back and forth for a long minute. Through all the talk, the male kept his eyes on the gear he tended.

Then the translator said. "You. Change. All. You. Sun. Not . . . hot."

So, they were giving her an answer. "I will change everything," Sandy revised the translation slowly, carefully pronunciation each word. "Because of me, the sun will no longer shine."

All four cats swung their heads back and forth.

"I'll take that for a yes."

That got her a gentle cuff from the speaking one.

"Yes."

"Yes."

Sandy sighed. So once again, a change agent was taking it in the balls. It was tempting to attempt a long philosophical discussion of just how they'd kidnapped the wrong person. That Sandy and the humans weren't the ones barreling down on them with murder in their eyes, but Sandy doubted the limited vocabulary that she shared with this one cat would do her much good.

Next time I come down here, I bring one racy computer with all the bells and whistles and all the languages that Nelly has translated.

Of course, a fat lot of help that future equipment load out was doing her right now.

Penny, Steve, where are my damn Marines? You said I had just as heavy a detachment as Kris Longknife would have had. So, would you really have let the princess sweat this long in a stinking, damp hole that looks ready to cave in any minute?

19

Penny stood on the steps of the command center. She'd called in the world. It was a real hoot to watch the world come running.

A few miles away was a very long runway. It was now cycling longboats through it at a prodigious pace. First, one shuttle would land and taxi around the apron to a stop. By the time Marines had piled out of it and jumped aboard small wheeled transports they'd brought so they could race for Penny's location, three more longboats were down, and a fifth would land as the first taxied out. While the sixth was on approach, the first would start its takeoff run.

There were never more than five shuttles on the ground at any one time.

Admiral Drago was not only dropping two reinforced Marine battalions, but a serious Navy contingent as well. Communications, medical, technical, whatever it took to support and feed this army was landing and moving out with the efficiency that only a highly-advanced civilization can bring to the organization and application of violence.

Hopefully it doesn't come to that.

Racing up the road from town was a different and definitely less well-organized effort.

The first to arrive was a police officer that appeared to be the sheriff of the district. She was quickly followed by the city's chief of police. On the very bumper of her car were three large, black rigs from which emerged cats, all in black jackets with sliver piping. Apparently, President Almar had her own investigative force and they considered themselves as having primary jurisdiction.

Penny, the daughter of two cops, understood very well how these things went. She turned them over to themselves and left them to debate the issues to their hearts' content. Maybe one of them was in cahoots with the kidnapper. Maybe none were. It didn't matter to Penny, none of them were likely to do anything good or bad while they argued who was head honcho here.

In the meantime, one of the rocket scientists had gotten hold of the engineers who built the command center. A small fleet of work trucks, rusted, bent, and muddy, rolled up to the bunker. Penny had a Marine captain take these engineering bosses down to see what there was to see.

Four minutes later, engineers and techs in muddy boots and loaded down with gear went running into the building. A few minutes later, the senior engineer was back at Penny's elbow.

"Hi, I'm Krysta. I can't say that I'm pleased to meet you, or you me. To start with, this is lousy ground," she told Penny. "Water's almost up to the surface. We had to drive pilings to get the bunker not to sink. How they got that tunnel to hold up long enough to pull this off is a bloody miracle and I spit on the goddess who accepted the offering," she said, spitting on the deck.

"Now, we can follow the tunnel, re-digging it and

supporting it as we go," Krysta said, "or we can forget what's down there. I strongly suggest we figure out where the damn tunnel is located from up here, safely on the surface, and follow it to where it goes."

"I like that," Penny said and as the locals deployed to do things their way, Penny hollered for a platoon of Marine combat engineers. She told the Marines that the locals had challenged them to a race to see who got to the admiral first.

Penny considered for a moment whether she could trust any of the cats in muddy boots not to pull something. Then she noticed the plethora of Marines or sailors now at nearly every cat's elbow.

With a confident grin, Penny stood well back and watched the mud fly.

20

B efore Sandy could make any more attempts to get the one that talked a smattering of Standard to explain why they had risked their necks to kidnap her, the male got excited about something coming from his board, and Sandy was shoved forward to a tiny exit. A short passage ended with her neck deep in muddy water. She stood in a small creek or bayou under a low overhang from the bank above. Two meters away was . . . something.

The object looked part animal, part mineral, with a bit of low vegetation sprouting from its top. Then the top lifted up, and Sandy saw that it was some sort of submersible boat. Two cats were at its forward controls, a third seemed intent on some propulsion system well aft.

Amidships was a void that two of the cats slipped quickly into with the flowing grace Sandy had come to expect from the cats. The other two held tightly to Sandy's elbows. The four of them then pushed or pulled Sandy aboard and let her plop onto the bottom of the boat with the rest of the bilge water.

The last two scrambled aboard, the top was lowered and secured. With a soft hum, the boat began to motor off.

Sandy had a sense that the boat settled even lower in the water. She suspected that the cats figured that being out of sight would keep them safe and sound.

I wouldn't bet money on that.

Mentally, Sandy began to count down to when these cats would find they were in a world of hurt.

Sandy had only counted from thirty down to fifteen when there was a thump. That was followed by a crunch and the boat made a decided lurch in reverse.

One of the cats who was driving raised a tiny periscope arrangement, then let out a yowl. She shouted something. The motor operator hit a lever on her device; it let out a loud protest, and the craft shot into reverse.

Only to come to a dead halt.

That stop was accompanied by the sounds of a propeller spinning, bending, and tearing off.

"Stop," Sandy said, from where she rested in the muck. "Stop. Give up. Live."

The putative translator said something to the others. An intense argument broke out. There were snarls and growls all around, accompanied by way too much claw showing.

There was also a clanking sound from aft, but it went ignored by the feline debating society. Sandy did not. She grabbed hold of a handle just in time.

Suddenly, the submersible's rear rose up. That tossed all the cats forward, landing them in a mass among and upon the two drivers. Sandy's handhold lasted just long enough to let the motor operator slide by her before she, too, was deposited atop the heap of muddy fur.

The boat was pulled backwards for a moment, then rolled over several times, which only added to the noise from her feline kidnapers. Then the entire arrangement came to rest right side up.

The top was blown open, up, and back, letting the sun in. The charges had been carefully chosen and placed. Sandy only had to work her jaw a few times to get her hearing back to normal.

She grinned at what looked in at her, but it must have terrified her previous hostage holders. Twelve big, beautiful Marines in fully armored play clothes stood, rifles at the ready, aimed right between the eyes of those seven cowered cats.

Penny was right beside them. She even had a blanket for her boss.

Sandy took it, wrapped it around her middle like a sarong, and stood up. Stretching out for what seemed like forever was a small army of Marines, sailors, and cats of many different types. Some of them had out guns; a few stood with handcuffs at the ready.

Sandy scowled at that.

"Penny, in case anyone has any doubt, these are my prisoners. Me, my, mine. No one else's, and no sharing. Have these Marines take them in custody. No one interrogates them but me. You hear me?"

"Perfectly, Admiral."

"Fine. Now, I want to get cleaned up and then I want a clean pair of blues. You get the word out to President Almar, Madame Gerrot, and that entire posse of cutthroats that I intend to have a nice talk with them just as soon as I can get back up there and it will be according to my agenda. Got that?"

"If they ask me the subject of this talk?"

"Your boss was too mad and you didn't ask," Sandy snarled, carefully stepping out of the feeble attempt at escape transportation. Two Marines stepped forward to give her a hand.

Once again on firm ground, she turned back to the cats that now were her captives. "Penny, have Mimzy say this for me. 'You are now my prisoners. I am going to have you separated because I want to hear each of your own tales. No one will harm you. Not a cat. Not one of these heavily armed humans. You are mine, body and soul. I *will* have answers'."

Sandy eyed the cowed captives for a moment longer, then turned to make her way toward a waiting ride. She didn't intend to study the faces of the waiting cats, but she couldn't miss the way the eyes of the police and other cats were just as downcast as her prisoners.

Yep, there's something rotten here. Before I let these cats out of their gravity well, I sure as hell better know what it is.

21

S andy got her shower first, with Penny serving as lifeguard. Three very intense Marines hardly left her sight, one looking in, her gun roving over anything that so much as moved. The other two looked out, covering not only the door, but every square inch of wall.

Not surprising, the shower was located off the restroom of recent sour memory.

The only person to risk the ire of Sandy's guards as she soaped up and rinsed was a doc who insisted on taking her vitals and checking out the blackening bruise on her face and neck.

"That's gonna hurt before morning. You want a bit of something for the pain?" he said as he concluded his once over.

"Not if it will impair my judgment," Sandy snapped.

He produced two standard pain pills. "If you need more later, you know where I live."

"Thanks, Doc."

Fresh blues made Sandy feel like a new woman. She started issuing orders.

"Drago, I want fast lift from here back to where I was this morning. Bruce, I want an armored escort, suitable for rapid travel through city streets and intimidating as all get out."

"They're already down here. I'll just have to clean the mud off of two."

As it turned out, it was these big heavily-armored tracks that the cats' escape submersible had run into. The monsters weren't amphibious, but they could wade in quite a ways and had done that, both fore and aft of the cats' quiet escape pod.

Sandy got a good look at them as she exited the launch command center. She also spotted the big-wheeled swamp buggy with a fifty-ton crane that the cat engineers had on hand to lift the fish up and out of the bayou.

"Remind me to thank the cats that helped you."

"I got Krysta, the senior engineer right here, Admiral."

Sandy was presented with a cat in tall and muddy boots. Her sleek black coat was speckled with mud and streaked with muddy water, but she was grinning from ear to ear.

Sandy held out her hand, and got a paw in return.

"Thank you for all the work you did to put an end to that noise," Sandy said.

Around them, cats were snapping pictures, and even a Marine was recording the scene. No doubt, posterity would long remember this day. More likely, some grandkids would be mighty bored with the repeated telling.

"I was only too happy to be called upon and able to handle this bump in the road of our relations," the engineer Krysta answered. "We are not all like them, tails between our legs, afraid of our shadows, ma'am. We really aren't."

Sandy nodded at that, but said nothing.

One of the armored Marine fighting vehicles rumbled

up and General Bruce stepped out. "We're ready for you now, Admiral."

"I have miles to go before I sleep," Sandy told the cat engineer, and likely the whole globe. "I hope your moon probe is successful," she added, reminding everyone that she'd really been here to witness a rocket launch.

Enough said, she boarded her ride and it rumbled off toward the airfield.

I have miles to go before I sleep and a lot of ass to chew before I get to the bottom of this box of cats.

22

Eight longboats launched out in rapid succession from the deserted airstrip near the rocket command center. Each was loaded with one armored infantry vehicle, four of the fast, light transports, and half a platoon of Marines. Sandy rode in the fifth one, Penny at her elbow, and seven cowered cats clapped in borrowed handcuffs, were a bit further aft under heavy Marine guard.

The suborbital ride was brief, and the noise level was not conducive to an interrogation. Sandy let her questions circle slowly in the back of her mind. It wasn't just these seven she needed answers from. She also needed to get the nine big honchos talking.

Really talking.

Who, exactly, were these cats and what was stroking their fur the wrong way?

During the shower, Penny had shared with Sandy the curse on the goddess that had supported her kidnappers in pulling off what was damn near a miracle. Not just a miracle that they'd succeeded, but that they'd all lived through it.

Sandy knew how close a thing it was. She'd been dragged through that tunnel, smelled the raw earth and oozing mud. She was not surprised that the tunnel had collapsed behind her. She was more surprised that it hadn't collapsed on top of her and the cat pulling her along.

Someone had coordinated matters closely with the locals. This time Sandy's longboats were vectored into the main airport. All traffic was being held on the ground or circling well away from them as they came in fast and braked to a halt before taxiing to a side hanger reserved for the local military.

Sandy assigned her prisoners in pairs to the gun trucks, but held the one that had answered her question and the white male for her own armored transport. The two of them huddled in the front of the rig, just behind the seats of the driver and two gunners. Eight Marines joined Sandy and Penny in the crew seats.

No sooner had the longboats come to a stop than the back ramp was down and the vehicles rolled out. The armored infantry fighting vehicles quickly formed into a line with sixteen of the gun trucks running before them, the other half following.

A number of local police cars and motorcycle cops led the way. They set a brisk pace that the track-laying armored monsters had no trouble maintaining. Sandy saw from the front viewports that they traveled a wide expressway devoid of traffic.

No one was taking any risks with her safety this time.

"They've got choppers overhead," Penny reported. "They also have aircraft orbiting above them."

"Let's hope they stay on our side," Sandy said, darkly.

"They better hope that they do," the gunner next to

Sandy said, grinning up through his sights of his highly-elevated machine cannon. "I'm locked and loaded on the nearest one, Admiral."

Sandy wondered how many of her young gunners had their guns aimed with just such intent. She did notice that the Marine did not have his finger on the trigger, but rested it on the trigger guard.

No doubt if he hadn't, Gunny in the back would have called his error to his attention immediately. There was intent, but there was also trained professionalism.

Thank God for the Joes, Sandy prayed fervently.

They turned off the expressway and sped through streets that were blocked off, with cars piling up behind police at every intersection. As they rolled into the plaza with the offices of the Associated Peoples rising above, General Bruce issued orders. Gun trucks and armored rigs circled the building, their weapons aimed out or high. Only the track with Sandy entered the basement parking area with the four rigs that held her prisoners.

They screeched to a halt near a bank of six elevators. Unarmed police held the doors open, then stood silently as Sandy, Penny, and her Marines streamed past them with prisoners being walked quickly among them. Elevators full, the police entered and used keys to see that the ride rose quickly to the penthouse level.

"I'm sorry, Admiral, that we don't have one of the two cats we picked up last time. I think they'd be really helpful about now."

"Why don't we?"

"Both were sent to Wardhaven to see the King."

"I hope King Ray finds them helpful. Don't worry, Sandy, we'll muddle through on our own."

Sandy waited after the elevator came to a stop. Gunny exited with four troopers. They swept the room, no doubt helped by technical specialists from the other elevators. Finally, Gunny waved Sandy forward.

Grand Admiral Maria Santiago of the Royal United Society Navy marched with intent for the small copse of trees that hid the table from view. The sound of gently falling water from the small glens around her did not calm her nerves.

I damn near drowned in mud and water today.

Before she reached her goal, the elevators were back. This time they disgorged only Marine dismounts. Most were riflemen who set about patrolling the area. Several were from a heavy weapons company. They scattered to set up light anti-aircraft lasers.

Sandy swept through the fake forest to find the nine movers and shakers of this world seated again at the heavy wooden table. They'd left the head of it empty.

Sandy headed there. She shoved the chair aside; she had no intention of sitting. Maybe she was madder than she thought: the chair tumbled over.

Sandy leaned on the table. "Why was I just kidnapped?"

Around the nine cats at the table, Marines filtered until twenty of them stood, rifles at port arms. Seven of them had a muddy and chastened cat handcuffed to them as well.

"Maybe you should ask the ones who took you?" Madame Gerrot said, nodding toward the prisoners.

"We humans have a saying. 'Where there is smoke, there is fire.' You and I both know that you threw a very tight security bubble over me. One that failed. Still, you protected me as tightly as you ever did one of your royalty. I want to know why. What were you expecting and from whom?"

Sandy's words were harsh and bitten off hard. They barked from Mimzy just as sharp.

I got to get me one of those computers.

The cats looked at each other, keeping their eyes low. None met Sandy's glare.

Finally, the one in the golden cape said, "It's them, the ones from the place where your Kris Longknife flattened the mountain and killed their beloved leader. These traitors are their running dogs."

If possible, the heads of the seven subjects of this derision sank down lower.

"I doubt that," Sandy said. "Your own media reports that those behind that iron wall have lost themselves in their own bloody problems. You have embargoed them and closed off all travel. Beyond that, I have the testimony of my own intelligence teams. Sorry, try again."

"It was an inside job," Penny added. "We are talking to two people at the launch site. They gave themselves up when everything went to hell. They are your own people."

Golden cape hunched over at Penny's answer, her eyes fixed on the table.

That was the way it stayed for a long time. Finally, Madame Gerrot coughed softly.

"You ask who might have done this. I think you should ask yourself who wouldn't."

Sandy allowed the woman a questioning glance.

"Those who are high up fear they will be brought low. Those who are low fear that change will steal away even what little they now hold. There are those who say their goddess is with you and that their goddess saved Kris Longknife from her attacker last visit. There are others who say their goddesses have declared you abominations that must be driven from the pride lands. Driven out or killed if you will not flee."

The old cat sighed. "Yes, there are many among us that are as hopeful for this meeting between two distant peoples as the eager young cubs that Kris first talked to. While Priff here," she nodded at the one wearing the golden cape, "fears that you will demand slave levies from us, some of our countries have asked for volunteers to work with you star people. Some of us guessed that you might need our labor to crew the ships that you might assign to protect the pride lands so we asked for volunteers."

Madame Gerrot turned to sweep the table with a quick glance. "My government, President Almar's administration, and that of five more were inundated with those willing to go to the stars with you."

Sandy used the prime minister's pause for breath to interject her own take on that.

"And how many of them would pack an atomic bomb in their luggage to blow up one of my battlecruisers?"

President Almar snorted. "Despite what the media says, no atomic bomb is small enough to fit in anyone's luggage, not unless you're letting them bring big crates aboard that weigh half a ton."

"If you truly become our allies, in name and fact," Sandy pointed out, "you may be shipping material that weighs tons. Besides, a shipment of meat to feed my crew might well be the size you mentioned."

"Don't we know the problem," Madame Garret said, taking back the conversation. "We have lived for the last fifty years with the fear of some rogue mailing in a bomb under the heading of 'agricultural equipment.' We have ways to assure that such a thing does not happen."

Sandy considered that.

"In humanity's long ago days," Mimzy put in, "before we outlawed the construction, possession, or use of atomics, there were entire security systems set up to prevent just what the Sasquans mentioned."

"Thank you, Mimzy" Sandy said. The computer's unrequested input had produced shock from all those around the table.

Penny, I got to have one of those.

Sandy paused for only a moment before returning to the matter at hand. "Back to the volunteers you spoke of. Assuming they don't bring an atomic bomb with them, or even a satchel of explosives, which, I might point out, would not get past our inspection, there is still the problem of intent. Madame Gerrot, you rattled off several factions among you that either fear or possibly even hate our very existence. How will you avoid them getting aboard my ships? These ships are complex machines. A spanner in the machinery might not kill us, but it would certainly inconvenience us. What if this sabotage occurs while we are fighting for our life against the murderous aliens . . .?" Sandy left the thought hanging.

"We have thoroughly investigated their backgrounds," President Almar quickly put in.

"Just like you thoroughly investigated the backgrounds of all those working on your space program?" Sandy shot right back.

President Almar and Madame Gerrot eyed each other for a long minute.

"Who keeps watch over the watchman?" the prime minister finally said. "You have clawed powerfully, opened our vulnerable belly skin. Let me offer a thought for all of us to consider. We could establish two, maybe three associations to check the background of each candidate. My government has three parties, and anytime we agree on anything, I am amazed. However, if the three parties were to organize separate administrations and review each candidate separately, we might indeed have at least one that uncovers an impropriety in an applicant's background."

The prime minister paused to let that thought sink in. Then she went on. "There is also the matter of us being flooded by volunteers. No doubt, even after we eliminate any that have the slightest question in their background, there will still be many competing for the few slots in your work draft. Might a lottery be used to pick the finalists at random? Lady Luck can dance a fine jig on the best laid plans of prey and cat alike."

Sandy found she liked the way this cat was thinking.

"How many of you already have voluntary programs?"

Seven hands went up, included Priff of the golden cape.

"Begin a triple check, using any source you think is reliable," Sandy ordered. "I think we will also be using your lottery idea for the final selections."

Sandy would also see that work teams were made up of cats from different nations. The more she scrambled the volunteers, the less likely she was to have bad ones in close proximity. Of course, there was always the chance of hires going sour once they were on the job.

We'll need to have regular transit between Alwa and Susquan to swap ships and people.

It had been a long day. Not at all the day Sandy had expected when she showered this morning. Her work done here. She, her Marines, and her prisoners were once again whisked to the airport and given the first slots on the runway. The climb to orbit was smooth and Sandy found herself back on the *Relentless*, sleeping in her own bed that night.

Seven cats, however, were quartered in the brig. Sandy might not spend her time finding out all they had to say, but she'd wait, with baited breath for the report from those who did.

23

"Penny," Sandy said as she attacked her breakfast in the wardroom next morning, "I am in need of a new commlink."

"We found your old one. It's still working, ma'am. Didn't anyone give it back to you?"

Sandy pulled the old commlink from the breast pocket of her blues.

"Oh," Penny said. "I take it that getting the old one back isn't the topic of conversation."

"Nope."

"I think she wants one of us," Mimzy said at Penny's collarbone.

"Something like that," Sandy agreed.

"We can *not* be swapped among humans," Mimzy said on her own. "Mother is very definite about that. It has something to do with us imprinting on our human, or maybe it's the other way around. Anyway, I don't think we would work well with anyone but the human we came awake with."

"I wasn't going to try pulling rank on Penny and demanding she hand you over, Mimzy," Sandy said, feeling a bit strange talking to a computer like she was a person. Sandy knew people who talked to their computers. They were usually a bit strange in the head. Helpful for what they did, but not someone you want too close.

"I don't know that we've got any self-organizing matrix out here on Alwa Station," Penny said slowly. "I can get you the top-of-the-line unit that we do have out here, kind of like what Granny Rita is using. Likely, we've got better than that now. We can also get you a skull net so you can talk directly on Nelly Net through your own computer. I'd likely add you to Mimzy's immediate access list so we could time-share. I rarely task Mimzy at anything close to her full capacity."

"I have my own special projects. We all do," Mimzy said. "Sometimes I work with my brothers and sisters on one project. Sometimes on my own."

"Well, Penny, yesterday made me a true believer. Get me the best that you can for now and get a signal off to Kris Longknife and Nelly, asking them if they'd mind shipping a kid here that Mimzy and I could wake up and I could work with."

"I'll have a call out on the next ship," Penny said, then paused. "Ah, when is the next ship, ma'am?'

Sandy winced. "I'd planned to send the King a report every six months or so, which means we're five months away from a mail ship." Sandy worried her lower lip as she mulled her problem. The less traffic back to human space, the less likely the aliens were to take notice that there were hundreds, if not thousands of worlds out in that distant corner of the galaxy just waiting to be plundered and murdered. For now, humanity very much wanted them all focused on this abscess of stubborn and victorious life at this end of the galaxy.

With a deep sigh, Sandy made her call. "Get me what you can and hook me into the net. For now, we hold the request for something better for the regularly scheduled Royal Mail."

"Aye, aye, ma'am. I'll get you the best we have on board now, then get you a better one once we get back to Canopus Station. As for the skull net, that will take about an hour in sickbay, looking at how your brain works. Bruce, Jacques, and I will likely all be needed to see that what we spin together out of Smart Metal is just right."

"Tell me when you want me. I'm not expecting anything to either set my hair on fire today, or haul me off to some muddy corner of that world below us. No. Today better be nice, quiet, and boring."

"Good idea, that," said Jacques, as he and Amanda joined Sandy's table.

"Anything happening down there?" Sandy asked nodding her chin downward at the planet of puzzling felines.

"It's really too early to tell," Amanda said, then glanced at her husband and got the giggles. He broke into a huge smile, part loving husband, but another part that puzzled Sandy.

"Okay, is there something you want to let me in on?"

Amanda got control of herself. "This is still preliminary," she said, then lost it again. "You tell her," she finally got out around rather adorable tittering.

"The cats are having problems about yesterday. Some of them."

Sandy sipped her coffee. "I should hope so. It can't be every day that someone runs off with the commander of the aliens orbiting in your sky."

"Actually, there is pretty much uniform agreement that

that should never have happened. There's a move to impeach President Almar for her handling of that situation. No, the problem is the secret recruitment effort to get people to work with us."

"A problem?" Sandy echoed.

"Yes," Amanda answered, now in control of herself. "The media and opposition are up in arms. Those that don't have a recruitment drive want to know why their country doesn't. Those that have one are being condemned for having it, or, in two cases, being condemned by one party for having one and another group for having it so secret that none of their cats got to apply."

Sandy quickly swallowed her coffee before she snorted it out her nose. She finally risked, "Damned if you do, and damned if you don't, and damned if you do and don't. Are you sure those critters down there aren't house cats?"

"I don't know," Penny said. "They sound pretty much like every politician I've ever heard of."

Sandy nodded. "Makes me glad I'm Navy. Okay, do any of you three see any reason why we can't just sit here quietly in orbit and let those cats do their feline thing?"

"No." "Nope." and "Great by me." were the answers.

"Fine. I'm sure I've got some boring reports to keep me occupied today. Brief me at supper tonight on developments."

24

S andy had a very quiet day. She got caught up on her reading, or at least put a dent in the reports everyone assured her she "really needed to read." She got through about a quarter of them.

Quite strangely, as it would seem, they pretty much agreed on most points. Kris Longknife had been handed three very tough jobs, and juggled them all very well.

Sandy had already gotten a good look at the fleet Kris had commanded. It was ship shape and in fighting fiddle. It was also a bit strange. When Sandy ordered up a sandwich to eat at her desk, the steward's mate striker who brought it was a Rooster. When she took a break for a walk around the ship, she passed sailors with accents from Wardhaven and Alwa, as well as Roosters and Ostriches. Kris Longknife had taken what was at hand and used it to crew a fleet any way she could.

She'd also built that fleet. Admiral Drago's *Relentless* was Alwan built, but Sandy couldn't tell it from looking at her. Like any of the Smart Metal^{TM} ships, there was a tendency at any time of the day or night for a bulkhead here or there to go missing or be added. Still, the general layout of this battlecruiser was the same as the *Victory* that had brought Sandy out. Its fighting gear appeared to be in proper shape, and its crew, despite their different number of fingers, quite ready to fight all comers.

Even more impressive, while building her fleet, Kris Longknife had also built an economy. The same lunar fabrication plants that provided the goods and gear to build ships also saw to it that the Colonials got the power plants, planetary ships and aircraft, construction and farming equipment that they needed to expand their standard of living from just making it to making it very well, thank you.

And then there were the birds. A quick call to Amanda brought a short lecture on just how much the Alwans were opposed to anything resembling an economy.

"Those that come to work for us don't even like to get paid. Most of them can't grasp the very concept that money, be it cash, credit, or pretty shells, has any value. We even tried minting coins to see if something they could bite and made nice noises when it was dropped might help them get the concept, but it was a bust."

"Then how do you pay them?"

"We print a catalogue of all the goodies that they like. They pick and choose what they want, and we tell them how many hours they have to work at this or that job to get that as a 'gift' from us. Gift!"

"It must drive a doctorate in economics crazy," Sandy said.

"Way around the bend crazy," Amanda agreed.

Sandy frowned, then flipped to a report she'd found, but didn't quite understand. "This Land Use Report. My fleet is homesteading the land down on Alwa?"

"Yes, that idea really took off. We're stuck way out here

on the other side of the galaxy, staring at the same bulkhead day after day, waiting for some alien to come along and either kill us or get killed by us. It's enough to send anyone to the loony bin. Since we don't have all that many loony bins available out here, the entire fleet was in danger of becoming one crazy place. I don't know who came up with the idea of working one week on and one week off, with the week off being dirtside at your very own farm, ranch, or whatever, but I think it's kept us all from coming apart."

"One week on, one week off," Sandy said. "That leaves you at half crew."

"Not if you invite Colonials or birds to join the crew."

"So that's where you get the polyglot crews I'm seeing."

"Yep, they join the crew, we get some leave. It's working out better than any of us ever thought it would."

"So, where does the land come from? Is there another catalogue that shows the birds what they get for this much land?" Sandy said, not liking the taste of the words coming out of her mouth.

"You don't know Kris Longknife very well if you think she would stand for that, do you? She's read up on when some of her ancestors were run off their land and shoved off to 'reservations.' No way is she going to let that happen here. Granny Rita's survivors got a grant to settle on some of the worst land on Alwa. They were just scratching out a living when we got here. Now, with modern equipment and practices, there are viaducts to bring in more water for that land, and more. We're eating much better. It was touch and go as the fleet started to show up. Yes, we desperately needed more ships, but whether or not we could feed the crews was an open question for the first year."

Amanda paused, a faraway look in her eyes. "Some of us

remember eating a lot of fish and some pretty strange nuts and berries."

"I saw a report on our supply chain. It didn't say anything about a potential shortage," Sandy said, not bothering to hunt up that report.

"Nope, it wouldn't. We're bringing in food from the Colonial farms at something like five times the old rate. Even the 'gentlemen farmers', as we call our off-duty folks, are pulling their own weight. Not only are we not going hungry, but fewer and fewer Colonials are needed on the farms. Some are working on the moon, others with the docks in orbit, still more here in the fleet. Oh, and a lot of the young Colonial couples are signing on to work with us dirtside to see that the fleet's farms really are productive. A lot of people are pulling together to make all this happen."

"So, I don't have to worry about this Viceroy hat?"

"Oh, I'd worry about it. Worry about it plenty."

Sandy gave Amanda a jaundiced eye.

"It's one huge, cobbled together construction with all kinds of feedback loops just waiting to throw the whole thing out of kilter and bring it all crashing down on our heads."

"So, it'll be a hands-on job."

"As we need more land, you'll need to negotiate with the birds. As they discover they like our stuff, you'll need to make sure we have what they want traded for our work, and make it a fair trade. That's not easy when no one here really knows what anything costs. Oh God, for a market economy," Amanda exclaimed.

"And that's not even discussing what my husband would gladly bend your ear about for hours on end. The bird cultures are splitting at the seams. I can't go into all the changes that have hit them since we arrived. Granny Rita and her few desperate survivors didn't make a dent on this planet. Us. We may not be nearly as numerous as we could be, but our trading goods are making all kinds of changes. Just the rapid communications our commlinks provide is changing these birds from 'I'll see you this afternoon,' to 'I can find time for you at 3:15.' Imagine jumping from the stone age to the 24th century in one generation."

"Frightening," Sandy said.

"A lot of the birds are really getting in with us. A lot of others are getting frightened. Yep, Kris minded the store real good."

"But now the store is mine to mind."

"Very much."

"Thank you."

Amanda left Sandy staring at the overhead.

How is a mere mortal woman to fill the shoes of a demigod Longknife?

25

For the next two days, Sandy immersed herself in the study of the many strange aspects of the new command she'd been handed. What King Raymond told her was a whale of a lot different from the reports on her desk and the conversations she had with Admiral Drago and Penny, as well as with Amanda and Jacques.

Then the fun really started.

She had made it a practice of eating breakfast and dinner with her team. It was good way of getting both food, information, and some human contact into a day that was often scant on the last. She, Admiral Drago, and her two intelligence types had taken over a small table in the wardroom, ordered their dinner, and had just began to enjoy it.

The two civilians were late, something they rarely allowed to happen.

They both arrived out of breath.

"It's happening!" Amanda said.

"Then order something before you let me in on what has

you so breathless," Sandy ordered softly. They were, after all, civilians.

A steward's mate, this time an Ostrich, took their orders. Even as the bird turned to fill them, Jacques started his report.

"Governments have been facing votes of no confidence all day. Two fell, including that golden caped one you had so much trouble with, Priff."

"She was a pain in the butt, but I didn't think that rated her being thrown out of a job," Sandy said.

"We're not sure. Her government was running one of the secret recruiting programs. It seems their censors were doing a good job of keeping it a secret. Keeping it a secret from everyone in her country, but her own party was the reason for the vote. At least, that is the announced reason. We're not sure that's the real reason. This is kind of like coming in for the last thirty minutes of a five hour movie. We don't know the half of what's making things move. Anyway, she's out. President Almar survived a vote for impeachment by a single vote in her lower house, and they promptly passed a bill to cancel the program. However, the upper house voted and passed a bill to keep the program and make it open to all."

Sandy rolled her eyes at the overhead. "I am so glad I'm Navy. I'd never want to be a politician," she prayed fervently.

"Yes," Amanda said with a wide, toothy grin, "oh royal Viceroy of Alwa."

Sandy threw the lovely woman a dirty look. Amanda let it slide off her with a lovely shrug.

"While the politicians are chasing their tails, verbally and otherwise," Admiral Drago said, dryly, "the fleet is getting offers to replenish our larders. We are running low on fresh meat, fruit, and vegetables. A fleet must eat."

Sandy sighed. "Good point, but can we eat their food? Assuming we can, can we trust what they ship up to us not to be poisoned? Oh, and can we pay for it?"

Drago nodded. "Madame Gerrot and President Almar threw a victory banquet in Kris's honor after we won that battle here. We survived the chow just fine. As for paying for it, word is, several governments are willing to pick up the tab as a Thank You for saving their necks or something. If you're willing to go along with this, I'll have our medical teams work closely with the Supply Department to assure we get stuff we can eat and to make sure it isn't tainted."

Sandy made a face at the perfectly square meatloaf and powdered mashed potatoes. "See if you can do that," Sandy said, "I am getting tired of this. The vegetables look like they've been frozen since the last Ice Age."

"We'll see if we can't have steaks on the menu tomorrow," Drago promised.

Penny got that far-away look on her face that Sandy had learned to recognize as her in an intense talk with Mimzy. Sandy had spent a long hour in sickbay and now wore a skull harness that itched maddeningly at times. The ships' docs were pretty sure it was all in her head, but that was the point. It was her head that was itching.

Hopefully, it would go away over time.

Whatever had Penny mentally away from the table didn't require Nelly Net. After a few moments, she cleared her throat. "Admiral Santiago, President Almar and Prime Minister Gerrot request a meeting with you."

"Will it just be them?" Sandy asked.

"There are three or four other chiefs of state who would like to be included, if you're willing to talk to them. They are all presidents or prime ministers who survived the turmoil of the last few days."

Sandy thought about matters for a minute. "Where do they want to meet?"

Penny took only a moment to answer. "Wherever you wish, Admiral."

Sandy grinned. "They can learn, these cats. Okay, this time they come to me. Admiral Drago, how many admirals' barges do you have?"

"Three."

"Tell our long-tailed friends to select three convenient meeting places for the five or six of them and we will pick them up. The next meeting will take place in orbit. Amanda, Jacques, do you have some photos of what Viceregal pomp and circumstances might look like on this planet?"

The two exchanged glances, then grinned from ear to ear. "Yes, ma'am. Are you thinking of decking the *Relentless* out like a seriously pompous feline palace?" Jacques asked.

"I'm thinking about doing something serious to the bow on Kiel Station's A Deck. Mimzy, how about you and your family doing some real interesting Smart Metal remodeling?" Sandy said.

"Mother was just talking to us kids before she left about how you humans weren't really taking advantage of all that Smart Metal allowed. We have some ideas."

"Take a look at what passes for the best in feline palaces, then surprise me with what you can do. Use the meteorite catcher on Kiel Station to add whatever you want to A Deck."

Every ship had a reinforced bow to catch the dust that littered space. Now that Kiel Station was no more to travel the void, it hardly needed a dust catcher.

"How far can we extend it?" came from Jacques's computer.

"As much as you want, just so long as it's safe," Sandy said firmly.

"Oh, it will be safe."

Sandy probably should have added a few more guidelines and restrictions. In her own defense, she would later point out, she was just getting used to working with super computers that inherited the Magnificent Nelly's sense of humor and grandiosity.

Clearly, she had a lot to learn.

26

Sandy's lunch at her desk the next day was interrupted by Penny. "Admiral, you might want to see what Mimzy and the gang have done to the forward section of Kiel Station."

Said admiral put down her sandwich, first bite not yet taken, and eyed her chief intelligence officer for alien life forms. "And just why must I see what your computers have done before I host our fine furry friends this evening? How are preparations going for the sit-down supper?"

"They're going fine, ma'am, although I still think that your tummy is in for an unpleasant surprise. They take their meat raw, you know, and the closer to the bone, the better."

Sandy's stomach did lurch at the visual, but she held herself steady. "If we are to be allies, we will have to accommodate each other. Certainly, sharing a meal is the least we can do."

"If you say so, ma'am, but don't be surprised if the cats pass on your dinner invite. They don't much care for the smell of our burned meat and I, for one, will be eating my steak medium-well."

Sandy had been given this warning several times. She'd just have to wait and see how it all went down.

"Now, about Kiel's forward section?"

"Yes, ma'am. You've really got to see it to believe it."

So, on an empty stomach, Sandy followed Penny up to Kiel Station's A deck. It didn't look all that different.

"We've sprouted a small pier from here forward," Penny explained. "We'll have the admiral's barges dock on them, so it will be a short walk to your Viceregal palace. We intend to line the pier and stairs up to A Deck with Marines in dress blues and reds. They'll also mark off this red carpet for our honored guests."

Here, the Smart Metal™ of the deck had been fluffed up into an extra-wide and very red carpet. Said carpet led to wide double doors in what had previously been the forward bulkhead of the station.

Two Marines opened what had the appearance of magnificent blond-oak doors. There were carved panels in each door showing hunting scenes. Duck shooting and riding to the hounds was something Sandy was at least mildly familiar with, but there were also panels devoted to hunting boar with spears, taking down huge cattle with lances, and bow deer hunting. A couple of panels even showed several forms of fishing.

The doors were tall and wide. They had plenty of room for panels.

How atavistic, but not a bad hint to our new friends of where we come from.

Sandy stepped through the door and nearly had to grab for the door jam.

"Damn," was all she could whisper as she fought vertigo.

"Yeah," Penny whispered back.

A portable space station and dock traveled condensed

down tight. Only when you needed it, would it expand out into a full-size base. In theory, Sandy knew that the fully operational Kiel Station had a circumference of two kilometers. Most days, it didn't matter. A Deck might have a tall overhead, but there was B Deck and a whole lot above it. The horizon was always just a short walk away.

Suddenly, Sandy was staring up at the entire length of A Deck as it wrapped around itself and came back to meet her. Now on A Deck it was a good quarter kilometer of grassy plain before you got to the forward bulkhead. It was that forward bulkhead that stole Sandy's breath away. It was as transparent as glass. The admiral stared straight out at the void of space, sprinkled with the occasional star. Five hundred kilometers beneath them, Sasquan showed in all the blues, greens, and other colors of a living planet.

"I wonder if the cats have ever seen how small their planet looks like from up here?" Penny whispered.

"If not, they are in for an experience."

Slowly, Sandy took in all that Nelly's kids had done, and it did take a while. This end of A Deck now looked very much like a wide, grassy savannah. Here and there it was dotted by clumps of trees and flowing water.

"I wonder how they're going to take to looking up two klicks to see a waterfall flowing up," Penny said, through a grin.

"As I said, they are in for an experience."

As if the deck above and the void before Sandy was not enough, as she walked out into the quarter klick or so of grasslands between the wide doors and the bubble at the bow, her eyes were drawn back to what the computers had done to the actual bulkhead of the station. Now, starting some ten meters above A Deck was a huge circular mirror that stretched for almost the rest of the two kilometers before petering out ten meters from the A Deck again.

It reflected back the stars and even had a view of half of Sasquan rotating around it.

Sandy again had to pause. She fixed her gaze on a clump of trees where a table stood waiting and held herself very still while her inner ear adjusted to what was going on around it.

"Wow," she said.

"Aren't you glad you're getting adjusted to this now, and not when you've got cats at your elbow?" Penny said.

"Yes. Speaking of having someone at an elbow, we might want to have each of our guests have someone at their elbow. I'd planned to wait for them at the table, but I think I'd better greet them as they exit the barges. You and Masao, me, and Admiral Drago." Sandy paused for a second. "Amanda and Jacques. Yes, that will do it. Let's have the cats get used to us having men at our negotiating table. I'm not sure I like their 'one sex rules it all' kind of way."

"More changes?" Penny said.

"If these six can't stand the heat, they need to get out of the kitchen."

"I've heard that advice before," the intel chief answered.

"Oh, you better warn General Bruce. I suspect his Marines that provide the honor guard from here to the table will need to get acclimatized as well."

"He's got The Word. He'll have them up here in an hour."

"Right, his computer is monitoring your computer and knows what we're doing, right?"

"Yes, ma'am."

Sandy frowned for a moment. "How does Masao take to having your relationship on net?"

"Mimzy knows that we humans need our privacy, and I have a lovely tea cup that she fits into just perfectly at times."

"I hate that tea cup," Mimzy said. "When have I ever told on you? I'm not nearly as bad as my mother. What she does to Kris Longknife is a pure scandal."

"There are some real joys to having a Nelly-class computer," Penny said, grinning.

"I can't say that I haven't been warned," Sandy muttered, only half to herself. "Oh, and Penny, thanks for the heads up. I never would have thought that my, ah . . ."

"Turning us loose to surprise you," Mimzy suggested.

"Just so," Sandy said. "You most definitely have surprised me. Oh, and this is safe?"

"We can patch any hole with no problem, but don't worry. It would take a major hit before you'd even know it happened."

"Thank you, Mimzy," Sandy said. "Thank you and all of your siblings. This should certainly impress our visitors from down below."

27

S andy's plan to surprise the cats got off to a rocky start. The cats had a surprise of their own. The five or six world leaders turned into ten and they wanted to bring along staff, advisors and, in a few cases, opposition leaders as observers. That raised the total to something like sixty cats all told.

Grand Admiral Sandy Santiago frowned at this development, then added three liberty launches to the transportation mission and drafted General Bruce and three more officers, balanced by sex, into her greeting committee.

She made sure all of them were in spidersilks. "I don't know how this is going to go down, but I don't want any human blood on the deck."

"Understood, Admiral," Penny said. "Oh, should I expand the table?"

Sandy got a cat-that-got-way-too-much-cream grin on her face. "Nope. We'll do it while they're looking."

"After all they will have seen before they get to the table, how impressive will that be?"

Sandy shrugged. "They don't know that we threw this all together in a day, do they?"

"No," Penny said, stretching out the two letters. "You may have a point."

Sandy still had the admiral's barges dock at the small pier. The liberty launches with the mob got a more plebeian greeting at a new dock a quarter kilometer up A Deck. Sandy expected that to add to the fun.

It did.

The meet and greet at the dock went as Sandy planned. She paired off with President Almar, Admiral Drago offered Madame Gerrot an arm. She gave it a puzzled look. When he raised his elbow a bit, she got the idea and slipped her own arm in his. Down the line, the other men did likewise to the female cat they were assigned to.

The walk down the red carpet, up the short stairs to A Deck, and then down more red carpet toward the waiting double doors started smoothly, then came to a sudden halt.

President Almar caught sight of her staff people walking down toward them on the round A Deck.

"What?"

"Space has no gravity," Sandy said. "You may have noticed as your barge came in to dock, that you seemed lightheaded for a bit."

Almar glanced around. "Some of us were rather disturbed."

"We did our best to make sure you were either under the gees of acceleration or docked with only a very brief time in free fall. We had our best pilots taking care of you."

"Thank you," seemed to have a lot of "I think," appended to it non-verbally. "Some of my scientists told me something like this. I don't think I believed them until now."

Sandy went on with her explanation. "This space station

is huge. It rotates slowly and the centripetal force gives us a sense of down. There are some problems with that down, for example, you are looking up at people that seem to be walking down from the overhead who feel that down is directly under them. Here, where we stand, down seems directly under us. If you could see through the decks of the station to this deck on the opposite side of the station, people would be upside down, but feeling a quite strong sense that they had a solid down."

President Almar spared one more glance at the approaching staff, and dismissed them only to eye the Marines.

"You have a lot of your warriors around us. Are you expecting a problem?"

"This is not a security detail, but rather an honor guard. They are in their most formal dress. If they were truly soldiering, you would likely not even see them."

"On a plain as open as this?"

"Yes," Sandy said.

President Almar looked around, as if to catch sight of a hidden warrior.

Sandy wondered if General Bruce had any Marine raiders in full scout camouflage, but she hadn't asked and didn't feel a need to know just now. They were coming to the end of the red carpet.

For a moment, she and President Almar examined the carved door.

"Exquisite carving," Prime Minister Gerrot said from behind them. "I should like to hire the artist."

"Yes, I had it made up yesterday just for this visit," Sandy said.

President Almar's head snapped around to frown at Sandy.

"I had all of this done yesterday just for this meeting. The artist drew on examples of how we hunted in our earlier years. I am told, some still do."

"No doubt," the president said cautiously.

At that moment, two Marines stepped forward, grabbed the bronze handles and pulled the doors open. Beyond it was a two hundred and fifty meter walk over grass that waved in a soft wind to a wooded glade where stood a heavy wooden table not unlike the one Sandy had met with them before. A waterfall thirty meters high cascaded down from pool to pool to form a small pond beside the silvan glade.

Behind that familiar sight loomed the dark of space. In it hung stars, and one huge chunk of a lovely green and blue planet.

"By my ancestors," President Almar muttered, to be joined by "Sweet Goddess," from the prime minister behind Sandy. There were other exclamations as well.

"Shall we enter?" Sandy invited. "You might want to rest a hand on my shoulder."

"Why?"

"You just might."

The president didn't need to be urged on twice. She rested one paw on Sandy's shoulder, and, uttering a soft prayer that the spidersilk armor was as good as its advertising, Sandy and the cat took a step forward. And a second.

Almar froze. The paw on Sandy's shoulder sprouted four long claws that dug into her dress blues. Fortunately, the spidersilk held, and the backing did its job of hardening behind it. The claws could get no purchase. Instead, out of the corner of her eye, Sandy saw the paw rise up on her shoulder, claws extended but going nowhere.

"By my ancestors, I have seen nothing like this," the president muttered softly.

"What has the goddess done? Where is the goddess?" Prime Minister Gerrot whispered.

"This is how we view worlds," Sandy said. "They are part of a vast universe, nurturing us with their life. You may notice that from up here, you can see no political boundaries. It is all just one world."

"Al, you said that these star walkers had changed us about as much as they could."

"Yes."

"You still think that?"

"I would love for some of my senators and representatives to see this view. Admiral, could you arrange for a regular ferry service up here?"

"That is certainly something to consider. As you can see, we have plenty of room for what we call restaurants."

"I know a few food providers who would love to set up shop with this kind of a view."

"We humans will want a few places for ourselves."

"It may surprise you, but we do have some dispensers who know how to burn meat. There have long been a few that feasted that way. It has been catching on since your Kris Longknife's last visit. It turns out that meat is easier to digest after it has been warmed enough. Those old crazy health nuts were right."

"Now, let us move forward so others can experience this sight."

"Yes, yes, we should," President Almar said, looking over her shoulder to where many of the extra sixty were being held back by Marines. "I would strongly suggest to all of you that you take a warrior's arm before you walk out here. It is not an easy sight."

Nonplused advisors quickly submitted to taking the arm of a Marine, be they male or female human, and the procession to the negotiation and dinner table got back underway. It was not without incident.

One cat lost bowel control and the humans discovered just how aromatic cat droppings were. No surprise, General Bruce was ready for this. A Marine quickly scooped up the mess and made it disappear.

Two cats lost their lunch. This also was quickly cleaned up. All three chastened felines were helped back to the confines of the more normal A Deck, there to await the return of their sisters.

With a lot of oohing and aahing and not a few calls on divine intervention, the procession made it to the table.

"I see you were not prepared for our delegation to grow. It was a last-minute decision on the part of our new colleagues and we felt it better to accommodate them, even at the risk of inconveniencing you."

"It is no inconvenience," Sandy said. "Mimzy, would you please grow the table? Will ten be enough places for you? Do some of your advisors want places at the table?"

"No, they will stand behind."

"No need for them to stand. We can provide chairs for all of them," and without another word from Sandy, the table moved forward, out of the alcove created by the trees and pond, into the savanna. As it moved, it lengthened, providing space for ten cats on one side and as many humans on the other. Between Sandy and the table, fifty-seven chairs, with proper holes in the back for tails, rose out of the grass.

Another cat dropped a dump.

"You can do this, like some warlock out of a nursery story to scare little children to stay in bed?" asked an incredulous Madame Gerrot.

"I can do this because of our science," Sandy replied.

"We have a saying. 'Any sufficiently advanced technology is indistinguishable from magic.' Since you do not have the technology, it looks like magic. I have this technology and use it every day."

"The goddess must walk in your train," Madame Gerrot said, reverently.

"Please do not speak of goddesses or magic," Sandy repeated. "We control more of the universe than you do, but we still stand in awe of what we do not yet understand. Wouldn't your ancestors who sailed your seas in ships of wood and sail find your steamships amazing works of magic? What about your aircraft?"

The two cats stared at each other for a moment, then both seemed to arch their eyebrows at the same moment.

"We want more of this," Madame Gerrot said. "What can we do to work with you and find our way to the stars? You have explained to us that our very existence is threatened. We've seen the wreckage of the alien fleet showering down on our planet, a summer of falling stars. We now have seen the wonders of what it is like to be you. Some of us fear that to tie our kite to your wagon will put us in everlasting servitude to you. Those of us here are not of that ilk, still we must explain ourselves to our voters."

"Then let us sit down and reason together," Sandy said, and waved an arm in the general direction of the table that had now ceased its perambulation.

The humans took the side of the table that faced inward. The cats were seated facing the woodland glade with its relaxing waterfall. Only if they raised their eyes did they see their planet revolving above their heads and the empty void of space looming over them.

Most of them stayed focused on those at the table or the

woods. A few, however, could not take their eyes off the other view.

At a nod from Sandy to General Bruce, the Marine honor guard marched off smartly. Ten, however, detached themselves from the rest and, led by a Gunny, cut their corners perfectly as they marched around the table to take up a position smartly behind each human negotiator.

Several of the cats seemed relieved to see the Marines leave, then changed their focus to the few that remained.

"You warriors move as one," Madame Gerrot said. "There have been a few great commanders who have gotten such obedience from their warriors." She left the question hanging.

Sandy chose to answer it. "We fight as one, under one command, with subordinates using initiative to blend all our effort together into a single, steel-clad fist. You have seen how we defeated the aliens."

"Yes."

Sandy chose to fall silent at that moment. The cats had asked for this meeting. The ball was in their court.

For a long moment, no one spoke. The cats cast furtive glances up and down the table. Those seated in the observer seats looked back and forth among themselves. Still, no one broke the silence.

President Almar was seated across from Sandy, Madame Gerrot across from Admiral Drago. Sandy had chosen to put Jacques next to her with Amanda at his elbow. Penny and Masao were at Drago's elbow. The four dragooned Marines, including General Bruce himself, formed the four outliers.

Mimzy, do you know anything about who these people are? Sandy asked on Nelly Net.

Columm Almar and the Bizalt Kingdom are reported to have less than a quarter of the planet's

PEOPLE AND MORE THAN A THIRD OF THE GLOBAL ECONOMY, ADMIRAL. IF OUR GRASP OF THE DATA IS CORRECT, THE OTHER EIGHT WITH THEM CONTROL ABOUT THE SAME AMOUNT OF POPULATION AND A BIT LESS OF THE ECONOMY. TAKEN AS A WHOLE, THE CATS SEATED ACROSS FROM YOU CAN SPEAK FOR OVER HALF OF THE PLANET.

AND CONSIDERING THAT WE FLATTENED A GOOD FIFTEEN PERCENT WHEN WE TOOK OUT SOLZEN, Jacques put in, WHAT YOU SEE IS JUST ABOUT THE WHOLE BALL GAME.

Sandy was very grateful for her net access now.

The itch is finally getting bearable, thank heaven.

Finally, Madame Gerrot cleared her throat. "We have long thought about what your Kris Longknife said to us. How a fractured world is not a world to let into space. Al and I were some of the few Sasquans to actually make a trip to space, and, no offense to Kris and her battered fleet, the view they offered was nowhere near as impressive as what you have laid out for us. Seeing our world now as you must see it, I better understand where you space people come from."

Gerrot nodded at Sandy and the admiral nodded back.

"What we are about to propose is not a spur of the moment decision. You may have noticed that several governments have fallen in the last few days."

Sandy nodded again.

"The media has mainly talked about these secret recruiting efforts some of us had and didn't have. Actually, there was much more going on behind the scene. We, the governments that survived, and some of the new governments now in office, have decided to form ourselves into a Union of Nations."

The prime minister paused to look up and down the table. Every head present shook in agreement. Madame

Gerrot went on. "We are not quite sure how this union will work. Its design is still a work in progress. However, if we are to stand our ground against the murderous aliens and stand tall among you benevolent aliens," here the old cat did not flinch, "then the cats of our world must learn to stand together, not bicker and bite like cubs in their mother's den. You will forgive me if I say, this is not something we have a lot of experience with. It is only within the last few decades, some would say with the advent of mass communications, and the outside threats that new weapons present that we have managed to assemble nations as large as the ones you see."

"You are not the first planet to experience this process of going from many to one," Sandy assured them.

"Are you offering us assistance?" President Almar said.

Sandy glanced at Jacques, the sociologist.

THIS LOOKS LIKE YOUR BALL, hardly needed Nelly Net.

"Say, rather, that I can share with you the many models that have been attempted so that you can chose among them to find one that fits you. Possibly, you may want to mix and match some parts of one with another part from another to patch together something that fits your need better than any of the ones I can show you. You might come up with something totally different. It's best to approach this kind of supra-governmental effort with the idea that it will be a work in progress. You'll want to review that progress regularly and refine your experiment."

"Ruling as a scientific experiment," Madame Gerrot said. "Who would ever have thought of that?"

"It's better than ruling as a dictate from this person or that," the human answered.

"Then let us get down to negotiating the fine points of an alliance or, if you prefer, conditions for our association,"

President Almar said. "At present, it appears that all we have to offer is food and labor. What we need," he said, his eyes rising to take in the vast expanse of deck and space, "is technology that will let us contribute to our mutual defense. How do we make this work?"

Sandy had read up on what were once called "Status of Force Agreements," accords that specified how troops from a foreign power would be treated in another country. None had been signed in centuries, but the idea was still stored away in computers. Her problem, however, went a bit deeper.

Not only did she need to make arrangements for how her people would relate to the cats while on their world, but also how the cats would be treated while traveling and working among the humans. No surprise, the sticking point was legal.

"If a human kills a cat on our planet, there is a blood debt that must be paid,"

"Does that death involve capital punishment?" Sandy asked back.

"Involve taking that person's life?" Jacques clarified.

"Of course," Madame Gerrot said, puzzled. "The family has a right."

That opened a whole new can of worms as the cat's judicial system was dissected and found very wanting from the Human Rights perspective.

The cats were no less horrified to discover that humans preferred prison time and rehabilitation. "It would be horrible to lock a person up. We would never do that. We need our time and space to roam free in."

In the end, they agreed to disagree. Cats in human territory would be under human law. Humans would avoid, whenever possible, going dirtside. If the cats wanted someone bad enough down there, they would have to give them a grant of immunity.

Sandy signed onto that, then thought of something else. "The cats that kidnapped me. What would you do with them?"

"They put your life in danger," President Almar said. "They owe you their life. We would have executed them already if they were in our custody."

"I think I've just got myself my very own herd of cats," Sandy said, softly.

"We have volunteers that we are in the final process of triple-checking their background. When they are ready to start work with you, what will you want to do with them and where will you want to take them?" Madame Gerrot said, taking the conversation back to practical matters.

"We will want them up here," Sandy said, turning to eye Jacques for opposition. "I think we should start them off somewhere in the station. We probably better begin with classrooms on basic issues."

Jacques nodded. "How to relate to humans. What to expect. Some basic language work. Oh, and an introduction to our laws. I'm sure there are a few surprises lurking out there. It would be better to get them out in the open before they get aboard ship."

Sandy nodded agreement.

"We can have the first fifty ready for you tomorrow," President Almar said.

"We, too," came from Madame Gerrot and several others.

"Are we looking at five hundred immigrants?" Sandy asked.

Madame Gerrot glanced up and down the table. Three

nodded their heads no. "Say three hundred and fifty now, with the rest coming along in a few days."

Sandy glanced Jacques' way, then at Penny. The sociologist spoke first. "I think we can put something together."

"My computer has already spotted empty space in the station," Penny said. "As we speak, it's converting it into quarters for the cats. It's on C Deck, so the gravity may be a bit lighter."

"We'll see how that works," Admiral Drago said.

"I've already got a lesson plan half developed," Jacques said.

Right, he's got one of Nelly's kids. They work fast.

Sandy took a deep sigh. "Then I think we have a deal. Penny, Jacques, I'm appointing you as main contact point for all things Cat. Admiral Drago, you're in charge of any efforts to have Cats supply us with the fresh food and any other supplies we need. You'll also oversee efforts to set up shops here on the station. Trips up to the station may be arranged by the local governments and will be met on a space available basis. Any problems, bring them to me."

You sure you mean that, boss?

Yes, Jacques, I mean that. If there are any problems, I want to know soonest.

28

Initial efforts to absorb the cats into the station routine went smoothly. The cats were a fifty-fifty mixture of manual skills, like machinists, mechanics, electricians and plumbers. There were also those with higher level skills like mathematicians, engineers, computer experts, and doctors.

There were also a couple of dozen warriors.

Those were bunked down separately and given extra oversight. After some discussion, they were added to the Marine physical training sessions. That proved interesting.

In a hundred-meter dash, the cat was way out in front. By two hundred meters, the human had caught up and by four hundred meters the cat had usually fallen out.

"They pounce in the attack," General Bruce told Sandy over breakfast. "They're not so good for the long haul."

Sandy stored that away for later thought.

On the rifle range, once cat rifles were brought up, the shooting was exceptional. Blindfolded, the cats could field strip their weapons as quickly as the best Marine.

"Of course they sent us their best," General Bruce was quick to point out.

Two nights later, two of the cat soldiers were found out after curfew. Sandy was awakened immediately. The cats had clammed up and refused to talk. Since they were from a minor country, Sandy chose to release them downside . . . at the space port established at the capital of the Bizalt Kingdom. They were picked up by local forces and marched off.

Sandy received a report the next afternoon. They'd been tasked to spy on the humans. They had nothing to report except what all the other cats had already reported.

After discussions with her team, Sandy returned all the trainees from that nation and had all the remaining cats given a demonstration of just some of the surveillance options open to the humans. The cats were quietly impressed. A few looked very subdued.

Several asked to be returned after that show. They were.

The other cats were finding it humbling as they discovered that the humans had little or no use for their present skills. Be they engineers, mathematicians, or plumbers, there was no work for them on Kiel Station.

"What are you going to do with us, have us sweep up the floors?" one asked only to learn that dirt was automatically collected and disposed of.

"But we do have work for you," Amanda pointed out, and had the station generate examples of fabrication work stations or lasers out of Smart Metal™ for them to work with.

More asked to return, but there were ten times as many waiting in line to replace them.

Then President Almar and Prime Minister asked for a meeting with Sandy and dropped a bomb, quite literally.

They met in Sandy's quarters on the *Relentless*. The

Forward Area, as it was now known on Kiel Station, was booked solid with over two dozen eateries, cat and human, already going strong with more scheduled to open. It seemed the cats couldn't get enough of Chinese food.

"It appears to us that our students have not been as helpful to you as we had hoped they would be," the president started without preamble.

Sandy nodded at Penny and Jacques who were seated at her elbows.

Jacques took up the response. "It is true that what they know does not apply that much to what we do, but we really didn't think it would. You have sent us very intelligent cats who, we think, will very quickly pick up the skills they need to work side by side with us."

"Let us hope that they can," Almar said, "but in the meantime, we would like to offer you something that you can make use of."

Sandy raised an eyebrow at that. "What do you have in mind?"

"Thermonuclear warheads," the president said.

Penny, get Admiral Drago in here soonest.

Mimzy already put in the call. He's galloping for us as fast as an admiral is permitted to move.

"Thermonuclear warheads," Sandy echoed, stalling for time.

"Yes," said Madame Gerrot. "We couldn't help but notice that your Kris Longknife did not use atomic bombs in our defense. Equally, we could not help but also make note of the warheads that the aliens launched at us as they came around the sun. Although they were mostly rocks, the attack did include at least a few that were some sort of atomic warhead. Some of the falling stars that made it to the ground were radioactive. That leads us to believe that you might not have access to atomic weapons."

Admiral Drago came in about that time.

DOES HE KNOW WHAT WE'VE BEEN TALKING ABOUT, PENNY?

MIMZY HAS BEEN STREAMING THE CONVERSATION LIVE TO HIS COMPUTER.

GOOD.

"Admiral Drago, take a seat. We seem to be having an interesting conversation," Admiral Santiago said, cheerfully.

"So I hear," Drago said. "Atomics are on the table."

A chair raised itself up from the deck between Sandy and Jacques, and the admiral slipped in at Sandy's elbow.

"The cats are offering to give us some atomic bombs," Sandy said.

"Thermonuclear warheads," President Almar corrected. "These are a thousand times more deadly than mere atomic bombs."

"Yes," Admiral Drago answered. "I've been studying up on those little buggers. Nasty things, you know."

"Yes. We have had some unpleasant experiences with them," Madame Gerrot said.

"We outlawed them hundreds of years ago," Drago pointed out.

"Maybe someday we can do the same," the president said. "Just now, it's not at the top of my to-do list for today."

"It's not easy, I'm told," said Drago. "It takes trust that the other folks with the big bombs won't hold back a few."

"Or knock together a couple quickly behind your back," the prime minister said.

"But you're offering to let us take a few of those monsters off your hands," Sandy said.

The two officials glanced at each other.

Madame Gerrot spoke for both of them. "We, the ten

willing to join together, have agreed that an attack on one of us is an attack on any of us. That in and of itself is a break-through for us. However, that leaves some of our nuclear arsenal surplus to our needs. Not a lot, mind you. We still don't trust each other all that much, but we've agreed to allow each other to inventory our arsenals."

The president took over. "We think we can trust the accuracy of the count and we are willing to give you twenty percent of our largest warheads."

"How many would that be?" Sandy asked.

"Two thousand," the prime minister said.

"Two thousand!" Sandy avoided shouting, but just barely.

"Of our largest thermonuclear weapons," the president put in. "We didn't include the smaller weapons."

DEAR GOD, HOW MANY DO THEY HAVE? Sandy demanded on Nelly Net

She got no reply, not that she had expected one.

Sandy eyed Admiral Drago. "Could we make any use of these city busters?"

Drago eyed the cats across the table. When he spoke, his words came slowly, as if he were stepping carefully through a minefield. "We have no doctrine for using atomics, since we outlawed them several centuries years ago. However, we do have missiles that use anti-matter warheads. We have to be very judicious in their use, what with all the lasers around, ready to shoot them out of space."

"So, you don't want them?" the president asked.

"I'm not ready to say that," Drago said.

PENNY, JACQUES, WOULD IT BE A GOOD IDEA TO GET THESE BOMBS OFF THIS PLANET?

TWENTY PERCENT! Sounded like Penny.

ANY REDUCTION CAN ONLY BE GOOD, SANDY. I RECOMMEND

WE TAKE THEM. WE CAN ALWAYS TOSS THEM INTO THE NEXT SUN AS WE GO BY, was definitely Jacques.

PLEASE DO, again was Penny.

"I think we can find a use for them," Sandy said.

"Definitely, I think we can," Admiral Drago agreed.

"Then we shall start shipping them up here tomorrow," President Almar said.

Sandy shook her head. "You don't ship them up here until some of my people get a good look at them and understand their internal workings. How to take them apart. How to put them back together. And when they come up here, they come in pieces. I don't want any of them going off. Oh, and my folks who go down there, they get one of those extraterritorial passes we talked about."

"Yes," Madame Gerrot said, "yes, you should go over them thoroughly and be trained in their maintenance. We will do our best to assure that there is as little interchange between our experts and yours, so there can be no problems between us. Still, we will give them a grant of legal immunity."

Sandy stood and offered her hand. The two of them shook hands with her and Penny ushered them out.

"What have I gotten myself into?" Sandy asked the overhead.

"I better get my engineers looking up whatever we've got on those things," Drago said.

"Mimzy has already done the research," Jacques answered. "There weren't a lot in the records aboard ship. I'm sending off a request to both Columm Almar and the Bizait Kingdom for copies of everything they have on their nuclear projects including the manuals for their nuclear weapons."

"It will be interesting to see how they reply," Sandy said.

"Well, if we can't give my folks any better information on the care and feeding of those monsters, I'm not sending anyone down there," Admiral Drago said, with finality. "I seem to recall that people died even when they were just working around that atomic crap."

"Yes," Jacques said. "Mimzy has already found solid evidence of that."

Sandy shook her head. "What am I allowing on my ships?"

"No," Admiral Drago said. "Not ships. Ship. One ship. No more. And not a ship with any cats on it either.

"Hmm. Good idea."

"Admiral," Drago said, "with that crap around, we're going to need a lot of good ideas."

29

G rand Admiral Sandy Santiago was starting to get anxious to get home. She'd left Alwa Station in some very capable hands. She would not have left it otherwise. Still, Commodore Rita Nuu-Longknife had a reputation, and nothing Sandy had seen in her short time orbiting Alwa led her to believe that age had softened the old gal.

Besides, Alwa was Sandy's command. A commander should be at her command. Though Kris had cleaned out the bug-eyed monsters pretty much in this section of space, they were still considered to be wandering variables, capable of showing up anywhere at any time.

Sandy was not the only one antsy to get back to Alwa. General Bruce settled at her table during lunch. "I sure miss Abby. How soon before you think I can get back to the farm with her?"

"Abby was Kris Longknife's maid, right?" Sandy asked.

"Maid and a whole lot of deadly things more," the general admitted.

"So that's how you ended up with one of Nelly's kids."

"That, and it seemed like a good idea to have at least two Marines with really smart computers. I worked a lot with General Montoya."

Sandy nodded. So that was how a Marine got into Nelly's family. He'd gotten close to one of those damn Longknifes and survived long enough to marry Kris's main sidekick.

Bruce and Abby aren't married, Mimzy told Sandy. Apparently, this head thing not only itched but also leaked. Abby says she's allergic to rings on her finger. Still, they're as married as Kris and Jack. Abby is Pipra's right hand, production scheduler, and expediter. I think mom did a good job of getting all her family into exciting places.

Can you always read my thoughts? Sandy asked.

Actually, I wasn't reading your thoughts. Chesty and I were following the conversation between you and General Bruce. Kris would often want Mom to brief her on background and I assumed you'd like this brief-ing. Was I wrong?

No, no. Feel free to brief me anytime you think I need it, Sandy said with a sigh, glad not to have her thoughts broadcasted all over Nelly Net.

Of course, if Mom gave you one of us, we'd likely be following a lot more of your thoughts. Not all, but a lot.

Oh, Sandy said. Penny would definitely be giving her a lesson on how to keep her thoughts to herself before Sandy would take any of Nelly's brood into her head.

Below, planetside efforts to form some sort of integrated economy were not working. The locals could provide food, manpower, and atomic weapons. Most of what they made was far too primitive to be used in any way by the fleet. But it cut worse the other way. Besides defense, the humans seemed unable to contribute to the local economy. There were just too many differences between the two technological levels. What gear Sandy had, she needed for her ships.

As it stood at this point, once Kiel Station exhausted its inventory of Smart Metal™ and reactor parts, they'd need to be resupplied by ships from Alwa.

Kris Longknife really had built the economy needing to support a fleet. Sandy was not ready to inject into the Sasquan economy technology that was easily four hundred years in their future.

Then Masao came up with an idea. His minor was in the History of Technology, and his computer still had all his course work on it. His computer might not be as fancy as Penny's, but it was no piker, either.

He and Penny cornered Sandy at supper.

"These cats were headed for their moon, right?" Penny said. "Kris Longknife challenged them to a moon race and they were racing right along when we showed up."

"As we both saw," Sandy pointed out, without adding a comment they both knew that deserved.

"When Earth humans went to their moon," Masao said, "they needed much better computers to do that. Faster. Smaller. Computers got a boost coming out of the moon race and humans never slowed down after that."

"Yes. I seem to remember something about that in some history class," Sandy admitted.

"I have checked some of the computing machines that the cats use," Masao went on. "They are still using vacuum tubes."

"What's a vacuum tube?" Sandy asked.

"Something that's slow, heavy, hot, clunky, and burns out a lot," Penny put in. "These folks haven't discovered either transistor or printed circuitry boards. To us, that's all ancient technology, but to them, it's just the thing to give their economy a kick in the pants and us a steady income stream."

"It is a money tree," Masao said, expanding the conclusion.

"Money how?"

"They have patent laws. If you have a patent, people who use your discovery, your idea, have to pay you money to build things using it."

"Yes, I understand that," Sandy said.

"We patent this technology, show the cats how to make things with it, and watch them take off with it."

Jacques and Amanda joined them at the table.

"I've already been investigating this," Jacque said. "They have some huge computing machines they use for census and scientific calculations. Some large companies are just now starting to control their inventory with computers. I can meet with some of the electronic manufacturers and show them how to do things better, faster, and cheaper with computers that they can make themselves."

"Not something like this," Sandy said, glancing at her new, smaller, and quite helpful wrist unit.

"Nothing close to what we have, but so much better than what they have now," Jacques said.

"You're saying that if we share some horribly obsolete intellectual property, their economy will take off and we'll get boatloads of local money to pay for food, clothes and other things we need from them," Sandy said, summing it all up.

"That's pretty much it," Jacque agreed.

"So tell me, my wise world-shakers," Sandy said, eyeing Amanda and Jacques, "who gets left behind to manage all this, make it come together without tearing this world apart worse than we're already going to have to? Not forever, but at least for the next six to twelve months?"

"You wouldn't!" came from both the sociologist and the economist at about the same time.

"You know any one better for this?" Sandy asked as innocently as she could fake.

The two civilians looked daggers at the admiral, then turned their ire on the two intelligence officers.

"It was your idea," Amanda spat at the intelligence officer.

"I don't know how to do it or that you would be assigned to make it happen." Masao pleaded for mercy.

"Some how. Some way. Some day I will get you. Watch your back," Amanda said in a deadly whisper, glaring at Penny and Masao. "Both of you."

Done with her dinner, Sandy left the four of them to sort out the guilty from the innocent. Her day was ending rather well.

30

A week later, matters had indeed sorted themselves out very well. The cats had produced their first printed circuit boards and were astounded to see what they could do with them. Admiral Drago, as Principal Human Representative, had signed contracts with several dozen companies. The signing bonuses would feed the fleet quite well for a long time to come.

More cats also arrived for training. Even the country that had been blackballed had begged its way back into the program.

"After all, if you humans are giving us the technology, we don't need to steal it. Besides," that prime minister said, shaking her head. "They could not make hide nor hair of what they saw. I swear it is magic. These boards, though, they are real."

Amanda was in favor of giving them lasers next. "Just the basics. The first lasers were more useful for data storage than weapons. Oh, and hormonal birth control. I just mentioned that and several biologists started taking notes. I think we may have lost the patent on that one."

"What about the males?" Sandy asked. "Are they still being left out of all this?"

"They are getting to them," Jacques answered. "This latest class had ten percent males. All college grads. It's finally dawned on them that if they send cats to work in human space, they need to bring along the men, and not as sex toys, either."

Sandy found that the cats were too much . . . cat. They were too ready to get into fights over what appeared to the humans to be the smallest of matters. Maybe the males would soften them. She shook her head. The sexist attitudes she was dealing with were totally illogical.

Among the final steps Sandy took before her departure was to transfer her flag to the *Birmingham*. Admiral Drago would keep most of his 4th Fleet; she'd only take BatRon 18 back to Alwa. Beside raising her flag on *Birmingham*, Sandy also declared *Yawata* and *Newcastle* as Special Weapons ships. They alone would carry the thousand nuclear bombs that Sandy was taking back to Alwa. Drago would have to keep the other thousand in storage here for now.

With those two ships off-limits to cats, that left the *Birmingham, Milan, Essen, Pittsburgh, Manchester,* and *Jamshedpur* to handle the cat passengers. Each took on two hundred, which increased their crew by half again.

And this introduced the cats to the birds.

Sandy noticed a cat sniffing cautiously at an Ostrich as she made her way to the wardroom the next morning. The Ostrich told the cat to get lost, something that only Sandy's new computer could translate, and Sandy left it quiet.

When verbal suggestions didn't have the desired effect, the Ostrich waved the cat away.

Wrong signal. The cat pounced.

Against a Rooster, this might have been a problem, but

this cat was taking on an Ostrich. The bird's kick caught the cat in midair with enough force to stop the feline dead in mid-leap and hurl it backwards. With feline grace, it twisted its body to bounce butt first off of the bulkhead. It hit the deck with a screech and raced away without a backward glance.

The Ostrich sniffed, and then went on about its duties as a Gunner 3/c.

Word got out among the cats that the birds were not prey.

Sandy was glad that the first couple of meetings between cats were with Ostriches. How matters would have gone down with Roosters might not have been so pretty.

With all things as well in hand as they ever were likely to be, Sandy had a final dinner with President Almar and Madame Gerrot. They spent it discussing matters in general and raising no new problems in particular.

They did enjoy Sandy telling them about how the Forward Reserve of the Kiel Station had come about.

"So, you were as surprised as the rest of us?" Madame Gerrot said.

"Yes, but I got my surprise well before you got yours."

"These computers of yours," President Almar said. "I got a briefing from some of my lead scientists on what your 'gift' of printed circuit boards could lead to. They were quite excited. So, hundreds of years from now, we can expect this kind of surprise from that which we are now creating?"

"Not all computers are as full of surprises as Kris Longknife's Nelly and her children."

"That woman is unique," Madame Gerrot said.

"No surprise that her computer is the same," the president agreed.

The next morning, Sandy's flag led BatRon 18 in its dive

toward Sasquan as it broke orbit and headed home. The cruise to the jump out was marked by intense training both for crew and passengers as the ships went through their battle drills and the cats followed their mentors in watch and learn fashion.

There were no more incidents of cats showing disrespect to birds. Now they walked half in awe of them.

Matters did get a bit tense the first time Sandy ordered the squadron to Condition Zed. The cats did not take well to the confines of the high gee stations. Then Sandy put on 3.5 gees and the cats understood that being confined was a lot less of a problem than being squished.

Matters were well in hand when the squadron jumped out of the Sasquan system.

Then it got dicey.

"Admiral," Sensors reported tersely. "We've got reactors in the system. And they aren't human. Ma'am, we've got alien raiders here."

31

"Comm, bring the squadron to General Quarters. Set Condition Charlie. Sensors, show me what you've got on the main screen."

Around Sandy, the *Birmingham* began to shrink. For the jump they'd already gone to a more battle-worthy Condition Baker, so all hands were conditioned to a tight ship. Now it got tighter. Sandy would wait for all hands to report at General Quarters before shrinking her squadron to Condition Zed – the war ready condition for fighting ships.

The main screen switched from a picture ahead to a schematic of the system. One dwarf yellow star had a large gas giant orbiting close in with small rocky planets further out before a couple of more large gas planets.

An ice giant was not too far away in case Sandy wanted to refuel.

That planet may already have been used for a refueling stop. Orbiting it were the alien ships, three dozen formed into four columns of nine.

No doubt, they had yet to learn they shared the system with humans.

"Nav, how soon before they know we're here?

"An hour, Admiral."

Which meant two hours before Sandy would know how the aliens responded to this surprise.

"Penny, are these more of those door knockers that got away from System X?"

Her alien intelligence chief was looking over Sensors' shoulders, giving his board a serious study. "I don't think so," she said slowly, then walked over to stand close to Sandy. Her words, when she spoke, were soft and for her admiral only.

"The four wolf packs that we destroyed at System X consisted of the standard, huge mother ship, something the size of a small moon, and hundreds of monster warships that weighed 400,000 to 500,000 tons with hundreds of lasers and dozens of reactors to power them. Short range, but you don't want to let them get up in your face and personal. These are things we've seen before."

Penny took a deep breath. "During their confab at System X, the four wolf packs came up with the designs for two new types of ships. The door knocker you've already met. They're something like the monster warship, but coated with a couple of meters of rock, say 600,000 or 800,000 tons all together with about half the lasers. They're slower."

"And these?"

"Are something else I was hoping we wouldn't be seeing."

Sandy gave her subordinate raised eyebrows and she hurried on.

"The aliens have been trying to make fast movers. The four wolf packs in System X came up with a refined cruiser model, kind of like our frigates. They have three reactors, two for propulsion, and a third to power about a dozen lasers. These are newly designed guns and have about the reach of our 16-inchers. We had hoped they were unique to those four bastards."

"Apparently not quite as unique as we'd hoped," Sandy observed dryly.

"Apparently."

For the next two hours, they accelerated at two gees toward the gas giant and waited to see if their enemy would choose to fight them or run.

As the clock ticked down to zero, sensors reported the alien cruisers had taken off for the nearest jump at an acceleration of 3.1.

"So these are their fast movers," Sandy said.

"Yes, ma'am. The question is, can they maintain that acceleration or will some of them start falling out?"

"Nav, lay me in a course for the jump.

"Aye, aye, Admiral."

"Now," Sandy said, eyeing the board, but talking to Penny. "Will they accelerate half of the way to that jump then decelerate to go through slowly, or are they headed off with their hair on fire to crash that jump at full steam? Nav, give me some options."

Jumps were tricky things. Treat them disrespectfully and they could throw you anywhere in the galaxy. Few ships made it back from a sour jump, so insurance companies insisted that merchant captains approach them rock steady and slow. Admiralties expected no less from their captains.

Kris Longknife, with the aid of the Magnificent Nelly, had recently tried some fast and loose jigs with jumps and it had gotten her all the way across the galaxy and back. Barely. She left with fourteen ships and returned with one, and that, the USS *Wasp,* had been fit for nothing but to be scrapped at the pier where she lay.

Since then, humanity had gotten better at using the jumps. It had to to get a battlecruiser fleet to Alwa and hold its own against the murderous aliens.

"Ma'am," Penny interrupted while Nav was still diligently working her board, "the aliens have figured out that if they hit a jump at high speeds they can skip over several near jumps and land much farther away. Where they go will depend on what energy they have on the boat when they jump. So far, they haven't figured out what putting a spin on the boat does with a jump. You need a computer like Nelly or my Mimzy to do that."

"Sensors."

"Yes, ma'am."

"I want to know exactly what speed and acceleration they have on them when they hit that jump."

"Can you get us closer, ma'am? It's a bit far to make that precise of a call."

"Comm, send to squadron. 'We go to four gees in five minutes. There won't be time to dismiss the crew to quarters to change. They'll have to strip down at their station and go into their high gee stations where they are.'"

You didn't want to have bra snaps or belt buckles digging at you when the ship hit four or more gees. It was normal policy to rotate a quarter of the crew through their quarters so they could strip naked in privacy before settling into their high gee station, ubiquitously known as eggs because of their shape. Sailors could spend days in them and the stations took care of all the bodily needs, both food and water taken in as well as what came out.

Today, there wasn't time for modesty.

Having given the order, Sandy called up her high gee

station. It rose quickly from the Smart Metal^{TM} of the deck right at her side. She kicked off her shoes as she pulled down the zipper of her ship suit, then let it fall to the deck.

Once the bridge crew saw that the admiral was serious about this, high gee stations came up and clothes went down all around Sandy. A few of the crew were heard to murmur into their commlinks. No doubt, their asides reinforced Sandy's order.

Sandy finished stripping out of her bra and panties, then settled into her high gee station. It immediately began to adjust to her every nook and cranny.

Or Granny. Sandy was reminded wryly that when last she'd talked to her daughter, there had been talk of a grandkid. Hopefully, she lived to hold that little one.

On Alwa Station, that was always in doubt.

Shaking off such human thoughts, Sandy focused on the board. The aliens fled at 3.1 gees. As she eyed the readouts, her squadron went to four gees.

"Penny, can the alien cruisers do more than what they're at now?"

"We've seen them hit 3.5 gees, but they tend to breakdown under the pressure. They can squeeze out another few more points of gees, but not much more."

The problem confronting Sandy had too many variables. What would be the energy on the alien cruisers as they bolted through the jump? How much could Sandy's battlecruisers accelerate now and still be able to decelerate and pass through the jump with the same energy as the aliens?

Sandy now remembered that all the ships of BatRon 18 were battle veterans, but they'd been built on New Birmingham. They might not be up to the exacting standards of those built by Wardhaven. She called up the skipper of the *Birmingham*.

"Captain, what kind of acceleration did your ship make on acceptance trials?"

"I think we did the usual, Admiral. 4.3 gees for an hour. Deceleration was a bit gentler."

"What do you think you and your squadron mates could make right now?"

"Admiral, on Alwa Station, we have to keep these boats in top shape. Our lives depend on being fast and light on our feet. Any problem we have, we fix. What we can't fix, the yard force takes care of fast. 'Fast in, fast out,' is Admiral Benson's motto, ma'am. These boats are in better shape then when they came from the builder. If you want to put pressure on those bastards up ahead of us, you put the spurs to these ships and they'll make you proud."

"Thank you, Captain," Sandy said. She studied the screen.

"Comm, can you get me status data on all my ships?"

"We're tracking it, ma'am."

"Put it on another screen."

Beside the main screen, a second one opened with all eight of her cruisers named. Beneath each were bar graphs showing engineering, weapons, and defense. All were well green with the exception of engineering. At four gees, the engineering bars were longer, with the edges tinged with a hint of yellow.

"You thinking of running the reactors hard?" Penny said, driving her gee station up next to Sandy's.

"Yes. But I remember how my ships fresh out from Wardhaven flunked out in their first fight when we asked too much from the reactors."

"And you're wondering if ships months out from their builders might be in worse shape?"

"Yep."

"You can trust what that skipper just told you. We may not be all spit and polish out here on Alwa Station, but our ships are mean and we keep them ready for a fight. We have to. We never know when those murdering bastards are going to show up. Like now. What the hell were they doing here? Scouting out the cats?"

"Sensors," Sandy called. "While we were tied up to Kiel Station, did we have full sensor sweeps out?"

"Yes, Admiral."

"If those cruisers had nudged into the system, would you have spotted them?"

"Ma'am, if they so much as sent a lifeboat through, we'd have spotted it. A month ago, we were dodging suicide speed boats. Trust me, ma'am. We keep a watch and we know what's happening in our space. Whatever those turkeys were doing in this system, they didn't take a peek at the cats."

Sandy had a strong urge to run a worried hand through her hair, but in an egg and making four gees, her hand wasn't going anywhere near her head.

"What are they doing here?" she muttered to herself.

"They might just be passing through, going from point A to point B," Penny said.

"Just coincidence that they happened to be orbiting that gas giant when we jump into this system, huh?" Sandy said, her words full of doubt.

"Yeah, that idea smells too fishy for me, too."

Sandy set that question aside and went back to her original problem.

"If we go to 4.3 gees, would we be showing them something they haven't seen?"

"I think we would, ma'am. I don't think we've ever pushed the boat to its limit in view of the aliens," Penny said.

"So, while they're in the system, maybe 4.1 is tops."

"Yes. Ma'am, are you afraid the ships can't hold 4.1?"

"Or just four," Sandy answered.

"Ah, Kris Longknife and Nelly had a backdoor into all the ships' systems. She'd use it at times like this to get a deep look inside the reactors' support machinery."

"Below the readouts on the engineering boards?"

"Yes, ma'am. She and Nelly could tell you there was a problem five seconds before you had it."

"And you're offering . . .?"

"General Bruce's computer, Chesty, and my Mimzy have been collecting the deep data from within the engineering spaces for the last few minutes. We can feed that data to your board."

This sounded like micromanagement to Sandy. Still, she didn't know how much she could count on these people, and they didn't know what to count on her for. Some captain might push too much to keep her happy.

Better I call it quits before we have a problem than some over-enthusiastic tiger pushing his equipment beyond its limits.

"Do it. If it's not too much of an imposition on the general, please have him actively monitor this. You, too. Talk to me if you see something I missed."

"Aye, aye, ma'am."

"Comm, send to squadron. Let's take her up a notch; 4.1 gees if you please. Any captain who has problems maintaining this acceleration, signal me immediately."

The ships on her list blinked their acknowledgments.

In her gee station, Sandy's hand got a little bit heavier.

32

As the maxim says, a stern chase is a long chase. It has been true since wooden ships sailed the seas of old Earth, pushed along by the wind in their sails. It was no less true now that ships had the power of a sun in their reactors and accelerated at forty-one meters per second, every second.

Space, however, is vast. Time passed and nothing happened.

As far as Sandy was concerned, nothing happening was good for her. Her squadron's ships showed no ill effect of her pushing them hard. Some reactors did creep a bit deeper into the yellow.

Sadly, the same high quality of performance held true among the alien cruisers. They stayed steady at 3.1 gees holding to their formation of three columns echeloned to the right. Not one of them dropped out.

Neither did they flip their ships when the time came to begin a deceleration burn. They arrived at the midway point where they'd have to begin decelerating if their commander intended to take them safely and carefully through the jump.

No flip. They just kept accelerating at a steady 3.1 gees.

"They're going to take it fast," Sandy muttered to herself. "Nav, get me an estimation of where they'll go if they don't slow down."

The answer came back quickly. No doubt, the navigator had been thinking just what Sandy was now thinking. "They'll hit the jump at close to 500,000 kilometers an hour, ma'am. That should throw them a good eight hundred light years."

"You know what system they'll end up in?"

"It could be any one of three. Maybe four. None have ever been visited. All I know is what kind of stars those systems have."

"Even mom was never quite sure where some of these long jumps would take us," Mimzy answered from Penny's collarbone.

"So, this time the aliens get to surprise us, huh."

"It seems so, ma'am," Penny said.

Sandy eyed the board. She was doing her best to catch those cruisers in this system, accelerating by one extra gee. Now, she was not likely to engage them here. It would likely be in the next system, maybe the one after that. She could accelerate harder here once the aliens left the system but that only meant she'd have to do some extra hard deceleration to hit the jump with the exact same velocity as the enemy had when they went through. Even if she did that, she'd still be well behind the enemy when she got where they were going.

She could think this problem through as many times as she wanted, but it wouldn't change the math of interstellar flight.

With a frown, Sandy turned away from the board.

"Comm, send to squadron. 'Have the crew rotate at their posts, half-alert, half-resting. We've got a long chase ahead of us.'"

She then turned to Penny. "You get the first rest rotation. I'll keep watch on these teakettles."

The intel chief wisely nodded agreement with her superior. She made the cover on her egg opaque. What she did inside the egg was now unknowable. Whether she slept or worried about their problem some more, or played a game with Mimzy, there was nothing Sandy could do about it.

Four long hours later, it was Sandy's turn to darken her egg and dim the lights. Going to sleep was another matter. She tried to sleep. It did not come easy. Even with her eyes closed, she could not get the sight of the main screen out of her mind's eye. It was very tempting to take a sleeping aid, but that was out of the question. Penny might wake her at any moment, and a groggy commander was not a good commander.

Sandy thought of happier times when no one was trying to kill her and everyone said the long peace would last forever.

Maybe she did sleep, because Penny had to wake her at the end of her four hours to turn the watch over to her.

"The aliens should make the jump during your watch," Penny said. "I've arranged to have the best team on sensors, from the antennas to the assessment group here."

"Good," Sandy said through a yawn. Then regretted it. A yawn at 4.1 gees was rough on the jaw.

"You get some sleep," she told Penny.

"You want another two hours, ma'am? It's a bit more than three hours before they jump."

"I got my sleep, now you get yours. Has anybody got fresh coffee? The brew in my egg is anything but drinkable."

The ubiquitous coffee mug could not be accommodated in a high gee station. However, if Sandy turned her head one way there was a nipple to suck water from. The other way was for coffee.

A yeoman motored her high gee station over to Sandy's. She quickly drained the dregs of yesterday's coffee, washed out the reservoir and filled it with fresh, steaming coffee. Sandy took a sip.

"There ought to be a way to mainstream the stuff, straight from the pot to my veins."

"I'm sure Mimzy could figure one out," Penny said, helpfully.

"Don't you even suggest that to her," Sandy whispered, then realized the uselessness of keeping anything from a super computer that was there at Penny's collar bone.

"It would not be a problem," Mimzy said.

"No. No. Forget I said anything," Sandy said. There were limits as to just how much help she wanted from those fancy new computers.

The watch was about as eventful as watching paint dry, which was much to be preferred over watching reactors boil over or explode. Sandy found herself wishing for a report on the alien's reactors. No doubt, engineers on those tubs were sweating bullets.

An hour before the aliens were due to jump, the skipper of the *Birmingham* called up.

"Admiral, my leading chief cruised her egg around the boat, and she finds the cats are restless."

"Restless?"

"She told them that we're on the pounce, but they don't

see anything. It seems the cats are very visual. I can't honestly say that the birds are much less happy to be in the dark. Even the Colonials are a bit edgy."

"Does your chief have any suggestions?"

"She'd like to pipe the battle feed, stripped of the heavy stuff and with a bit of commentary for color, through to every high gee station. She strongly suspects that even the trained sailors we brought from New Birmingham could use the distraction."

"It's not going to be very exciting. I'm looking at it and I'm kind of bored, to tell you the truth."

"I'm looking at it too, ma'am, and I agree with you, but we're old hands. For the kids, it's likely to be really cool."

"Are they still using that word?"

"How should I know, Admiral? You and I know what it means. That's all that matters to me."

"Have your leading chief put together whatever she thinks will be helpful, check it out with your XO, and mount it on the ship's open net. Oh, and pass the idea along to the other ships behind us. Tell the leading chiefs on the other boats that there's a contest to see which ship comes up with the least boring feed."

"Do you really want to challenge the chiefs, Admiral?

It only took Sandy a moment to recognize that inviting the senior chiefs to be creative was no less open to surprises than challenging super computers.

"You have a very good point, Captain," Sandy said. "Tell her to do whatever you think is best."

"I'll get her on it right away, ma'am."

Sandy heard nothing further about that. No doubt, the crews below decks ate it up.

An hour later, the aliens went through the jump one ship at a time, barely a second apart.

Sensors had an immediate report. "They were making 512,316 kilometers per hour at exactly 3.089 gees acceleration. Rock steady. No rotation on the ship."

That settled that.

Sandy now had numbers. "Nav, plot me a course where we go to 4.3 gees for six hours, then resuming 4.1 for six hours. We'll follow that course until we flip ship and begin decelerating. Let me know how much we'd have to put in at 4.3, then alternate as much time as needed with 4.1 deceleration. I want to hit that jump at exactly the aliens' numbers."

Nav had an answer back in less than a minute. "Ten hours to flip ship, half at high acceleration, half at lower. Our deceleration toward the jump will be about two hours high, one low. I'm ready to send the exact course to the squadron. We'll flip again and use their exact acceleration to jump through. Shall I send the course?"

Sandy frowned at the screen, now showing the high acceleration part of the course in red, the rest in yellow. She'd be hammering the ships' reactors hard. Would the rest at *only* 4.1 gees be enough? Lord, in her days in destroyers, a three gee acceleration was considered an outstanding performance from the ship's engineering division. Kris Longknife had jacked up the acceleration and the pressure on everyone. There were risks involved in this course. She eyed her board. It showed all reactors with plenty of yellow left, and the computer's continuous deep review showed no hints of impending failure.

"Nav give Comm your course. Comm, send to the squadron. 'A six-hour speed run at 4.3 gees starts in two minutes. Captains, please advise me of problems'."

Two minutes went by with no adverse comments and no evidence of problems. "Commence speed run . . . now," Sandy ordered.

Sandy watched her boards like a hawk as the ships put on the extra gees without fault or problem. The reactor cores took the extra plasma in, heated it up, and spat it out the end. Containment held and the cooling systems did their work. Three cooling pumps fell out, but three backup pumps kicked in without a drop in the flow of coolant around the reactors that, only seconds later, was fed into the reactors and superheated to plasma.

Here again, the Smart Metal™ made repairs manageable. The three balky pumps were dissolved into the basic matrix and reformed according to specs without anyone having to get out of a high gee station. Five minutes after the initial failures, all three pumps were back online, tested, and ready to kick in if needed.

Sandy shook her head. If the aliens knew what they were up against, would they call it quits? She'd seen the pictures from that horror house. If she stayed out here long enough, she'd need to take the trip herself, out to see it with her own eyes. A team of scientists had come out from Wardhaven with her fleet specifically on the chance they might get to spend a month examining the last remains of so many races.

Humans were curious. No proof to the contrary, the aliens were not.

Nor were they likely to change.

Sandy finished her watch with the squadron still going smoothly at 4.3 gees. She turned the watch over to Penny and dimmed her station. She'd done a good four hours of work.

She and Penny switched watches three times before the jump came up. Both were awake for that. The squadron's ships shot through the tiny pinhole in space less than a second apart. Each ship matched its velocity and acceleration exactly to the alien ships that had gone through before them.

33

N av quickly reported, "All eight ships of the squadron are through, ma'am. We've jumped 784 light years."

Sensors was only a second behind her. "I have the aliens. There is a lot of jamming, but I have thirty-six cruisers and they appear to be on a course to slingshot themselves around a rocky planet and shoot themselves off for another jump.

"Jamming?" Penny demanded before Sandy would have.

"Yes, ma'am. I've got the ships, but I can't read anything about the reactors anymore."

"Is one of their ships having an engineering casualty?" Penny asked. "They've blown themselves out of space a few times when their reactors were pushed too hard for too long," she advised Sandy.

The lieutenant on sensors shook his head inside his egg. Very carefully. "It could be the planet they're passing. It's making noise like an overheated gas giant but it shows on our sensors as a sold chunk of rock."

Time was wasting. An admiral had orders to issue.

"Comm, send to squadron, 'Set course for the rock, acceleration 4.1 gees.'"

A slingshot swing around a planet could give a push to the just as well as the unjust.

Once again, Sandy switched four hour watches with Penny. By the end of Penny's first watch, the intel officer was still puzzling over that rocky planet they were aiming for. "Noise. Nothing but noise off that pebble. No planet should be that noisy."

"Space is vast and full of surprises," Sandy answered, and sent Penny to nap.

By the end of Penny's second watch, the woman was downright paranoid. "There is something definitely wrong with that planet. Noise all up and down the electromagnetic spectrum. Nature just doesn't do that."

"You've spent too much time with one of those damn Longknifes," Sandy said. "You're getting as paranoid as one of them."

"Yeah, but it's kept them alive, hasn't it?"

Which burned Sandy. All too often, Longknifes stayed alive because a Santiago died in their place.

Sandy said nothing and sent Penny to rest.

However, her alien advisor had gotten her commander's attention.

Too damn many Santiagos had *died for the Longknife legend,* she fumed. Then came up short.

Am I about to add another name to a list with way too many already?

Sandy spent the watch studying the rock they were accelerating toward.

At the velocity and acceleration they had on the ships,

they'd have to nearly skim the surface of that planet to get every bit of the extra acceleration they could.

A planet that cloaked its secrets like a striptease queen in an overcoat and galoshes wanted them to get up close and personal.

Where have I heard that before?

Right.

The alien warships all full of lasers that you never want to let get up in your face.

Sandy slept on that thought and awoke with the absolute conviction that particular planet was not protecting its secrets for any good reason.

Penny had no pointed questions for Sandy as she briefed her before turning over the watch.

"Don't sack out just yet," Sandy told her intel chief. "Sensors, talk to me about that rock we're headed for."

"It's a rock. A big rock that has no right to be making all that noise."

"Is it inhabitable?"

That got Penny's eyebrows up.

"No ma'am," came as a slow answer. "Not unless someone's come up with an alien species that can breathe vacuum and eat rock. As dead planets come, it's right up there with the deadest."

"Okay, Penny, I may need all the computing power your Mimzy and Bruce's Chesty have got. Get me the skippers of the *Newcastle* and *Yawata.*"

"Them?"

"Yep, the cats are about to earn their pay."

As if Sandy didn't have enough suspicions dancing a jig with the small hairs on the back of her neck, sensors interrupted the discussion.

"One of the alien cruiser's deceleration is falling off

rapidly. It's down to 2.8. Now it's 2.6. Others are falling out of high boost. Four, eight, fifteen. Ah, all of them"

By the time the ships settled down, they were all steady at 1.5 gees.

"Interesting," Sandy said. "Very interesting.

34

The rock that held Sandy's interest kept one face toward them and the other face, the one they'd be making a close pass by, away from them. They could see a bit around it, but would only get a good look at that side as they sped by it at over 700,000 kilometers an hour.

That wouldn't give much time to sightsee.

Making matters worse, as they closed on the planet and got a better view around the edge to that other side, it turned out to have a huge crater wall shielding a vast bit of territory from view.

"If you were setting up an ambush," Sandy asked Penny, "where would you put it?"

"In that crater. Likely as close to that wall as possible to give you more time when you weren't in our view. That would also let them shoot longer over the far side of the crater as we're going away.

"My thoughts entirely."

"We could have our lasers ready as we go over the lip of

the crater," Penny said, "but I'm guessing they'll have tons of lasers firing back at us."

"Worse, whoever is setting up this ambush will have observation posts on the wall of that crater, picking out targets, tracking them, and getting the range dialed in just right," Sandy said.

"They could see us, but we wouldn't have any idea of what we were about to face," Penny agreed.

Sandy sighed. It was too late to avoid this. They had way too much energy on the boats. Still, there were several ways around this little problem. Which would she pick?

Silly question, the peace had gone long, but it hadn't dulled Sandy's fighting instincts.

"Comm, order the squadron to Condition Zed. Make sure the crystal is nice and smooth forward."

"Done, ma'am," Comm reported.

"*Newcastle* and *Yawata*, take the lead."

The rest of the squadron dropped down a fraction of a gee to allow those ships to move ahead. Once they were in place, the squadron resumed its steady 4.1 gee acceleration, adding on the velocity, relentlessly in pursuit of the fleeing cruisers.

It only took a few orders to the two lead ships and Sandy watched as a new window was added to her board. She spent a lot of time checking in with Mimzy and Chesty on exactly what she wanted.

What she asked, they provided.

How do you pin a medal on a computer? She would have to try.

Relentlessly, physics ruled this battlefield with an iron rod. Gravity now added to their acceleration, hurling them at the planet even faster than the outrageous speed their reactors had already built up.

With a close encounter only seconds away, Grand Admiral Maria Santiago gave the command that she had thought no human commander would ever give again.

"*Newcastle, Yawata*, launch nuclear strike."

35

Nine specially crafted Smart Metal™ missiles fanned out from the two lead battlecruisers. Mimzy and Chesty had specifically designed them to be quite unique. They accelerated at twenty gees, leaving the launch ships behind like they were standing still.

No sooner were the first nine away than another nine launched out, and then another. Five separate and distinct waves were soon on their way, rocketing ahead of Sandy's squadron. The missiles in each wave had been designed for a specific purpose and each followed different paths toward the crater and its fiercely guarded secret.

The first nine flew low. They had been programmed to target the lip of the ridge. By going low, they benefitted from its masking value that previously had gone to the aliens. If the suspected massed laser batteries were in that crater, they did not get a shot at this incoming death.

Nine twenty-megaton warheads exploded against the ridge a fraction of a second before they would have smashed themselves to atoms.

Instead, they blew themselves to atoms. Themselves and

the crater lip along with whatever observation posts the alien commander had stationed there. If the posts had any defense, Sandy saw no evidence of any effort to take out the missiles.

Evenly spaced along the lip, thermonuclear warheads converted the rocky ridge line into hell.

Just as evenly spaced, but offset to streak between the thermonuclear explosions, came nine more missiles, likewise uniquely designed by Nelly's kids. Humanity had never super-hardened anything against the electromagnetic pulse of huge nuclear explosions, but humanity had the skill to do it. In the last several hours, humanity's best computers had done just that.

Nine rockets shot through the potentially fratricidal effect of the first line of strikes and kept going.

These nine came in higher than the first ones. They dove over the lip of the crater. Again, just nanoseconds before they would have destroyed themselves, their twenty megaton explosions wreaked havoc on whatever lurked unseen inside the crater.

A third wave followed the general course of the first strike. These missiles were not only designed to be super-hardened against electromagnetic pulse, but their Smart Metal^{TM} protected them from the hellish fire and shock waves coming off the first line of expanding nuclear clouds.

They shot through the upper reaches of the raging maelstrom, then dove.

For a fraction of a second, they might have stood out on radar as targets, but only for a fraction of a second. They exploded two thousand feet above the crater floor, flattening everything beneath them for a mile or more.

This was Sandy's one uncertainty. How fast could the

aliens react? Could their computers quickly acquire a target, slave their lasers to it, then fire? It was impossible for Sandy to know that answer. She'd only find out when her ships streaked over the crater or when some lasers remained to shoot at them.

Wave after wave, second by second, missiles streaked above the rising nuclear hell before they dove to add their own line to the advancing wall of destruction.

Sandy's ships sped towards their rendezvous with what she was now sure was an ambush. An ambush she had tripped early. Ahead of them, now, a wall of nuclear hellfire rose up from the planet.

Close encounter would have her ships skimming the planet by a mere five hundred kilometers. At that altitude, the roiling hell clouds of the atomic demons should not reach out for them.

It also meant that Sandy's ships would have little time to shoot at anything that survived.

Assuming any did.

"Zero acceleration. Nose on to that rock," Sandy ordered.

Her squadron lost all acceleration. In their high gee stations, crew went from the oppression of weighing over four times their normal to weighing nothing.

Lasers were fully loaded. Half were at full power, ready to smash through armor or rock, if the aliens had chosen to dig their lasers in.

The other half were at ten percent power, with the ship's power grid ready to feed juice to them just as fast as they pumped power out. These would be targeted at anything the aliens left out in the open that hadn't been smashed by the thermonuclear attack.

At the speed the squadron was traveling, it would be

impossible for the human eye to spot targets, track the lasers in on them, then fire.

As much as it pained Sandy, she surrendered her squadron to Mimzy and Chesty for fire direction. The two computers were now weapons-free on both the *Birmingham* and the *Essen*, with the other ships' fire controls slaved to them, but with that pesky speed of light delay.

What happened next took less than a second. Sandy only came to understand it when Mimzy played it back in super-slow motion.

"You were right. There was an ambush waiting for us," Mimzy said.

"The nuclear bombs took care of most of it. From the partially wrecked equipment we saw on our pass, they had packed that crater with lasers just as tight as they could. Think of an dense blackberry thicket," the computer offered.

Having never seen a blackberry thicket, dense or otherwise, Sandy had no real frame of reference, but she assumed they were packed as tight as ready rounds in an ammo box.

"Some of the missiles must have either failed to explode or been intercepted. We hosed down the untouched areas. I doubt if many aliens survived. I would guess that if any actually are still alive down there, the expanding nuclear shockwaves will likely rip them to pieces or fry them. Likely both."

The computer paused for the humans to comprehend the full extend of her words.

"I don't think you need to worry about going back to finish them off," Mimzy concluded.

The bridge crew had fallen silent as a tomb, while the computer narrated what the main screen was showing.

Sandy hated to break that silence. Even murderous monsters deserved some respect for their slaughtered dead.

Still, she had a fleet to command.

"Comm, send to squadron. Course for the jump. Stand by to acceleration at 4.1 gees."

"Aye, aye, ma'am. All report course for the jump loaded. Standing by for 4.1 gee acceleration."

"Punch it."

BatRon 18 resumed its grim pursuit of the fleeing thirty-six alien cruisers that had been the bait for this trap.

36

I t quickly became clear that leading the squadron into the ambush had been the primary objective of the cruisers.

While Sandy had been concentrating on blowing her way through and past the ambush, the cruisers had adjusted their course. They were now decelerating at 3.2 gees toward a gas giant.

"Nav, talk to me about their course."

"If they can hold to this deceleration, they should be able to use that planet to slingshot themselves back in our general direction. They'll still be going awfully fast, ma'am."

Mimzy had her own assessment. "If they were willing to risk a very close pass, say skimming close enough to get warmed by the uppermost atmosphere, they might get closer to us. If they deployed even the most rudimentary sort of air brakes, they could slow themselves down and if they vector their thrust just right, they could be headed very much in our direction."

"I wonder what they'll do now?" Penny asked.

Sandy could only shake her head. What would she do if her plan had been busted up as bad as this one had?

For now, she had orders to give.

"Comm, send to squadron 'Change course for gas giant. Set Condition Charlie. Deceleration 1.25 gee on my mark. Release one quarter of the crew to quarters to get cleaned up. Rotate every thirty minutes'."

"All ships acknowledge, ma'am."

"Send my mark."

Suddenly, Sandy felt so light she could fly. After so long under punishing gees, a mere 1.25 gees was easy. Her joy was short lived as she also felt the dirt and grime of the last couple of days. She was glad this contraption made sure no one could smell her.

"Penny, you take the first break. I'll take the watch here."

"Admiral, it will be at least an hour before we see how they're reacted to what we did back there. Would you please go first? I'd hate to have to haul you out of the shower if something came up fifty-five minutes from now."

With the lid off of her egg, Sandy could run a worried hand through her hair. It was damp and oily from the sweat she'd worked up during the long pursuit and smashing the ambush.

"Okay, you win this one, Captain."

"Good Admiral, now go get cleaned up. I can smell you from here."

Sandy made a face at her intel chief, but motored the egg off the bridge and into her quarters. That shower was as close as she'd been to ecstasy in years.

Sandy pulled on fresh clothes and returned to the bridge. There, the eggs had vanished back into the deck, leaving the crew standing their watches in very much undress nothing.

Penny greeted Sandy with a smile, a ham and cheese sandwich, and a steaming mug of coffee.

"You stink," Sandy said. "Go shower with Masao. Think of how much water we'll save."

"It's all recycled or burned as fuel," Penny said, but with a smile in her boyfriend's direction, they strode quickly from the bridge.

Sandy was pretty sure that something was coming up there.

As she munched her sandwich, Sandy studied the surviving aliens in the system. They were still braking toward the gas giant at 3.2 gees.

"Sensors, can you tell me anything about that rock we just plastered?"

"We aren't getting any more jamming, I can definitely report that, Admiral. As for what's left, it's hard to tell. The noise from those thermonuclear explosions has pretty much settled down. I cannot pick up any reactors, nor are any capacitors making noise. Ma'am, it sounds like a very dead rock should sound."

Sandy thought for a moment about any intelligent life that might be struggling to survive in that living hell she'd created back there. Then she reflected on what they intended to do to her and her squadron.

She thought no more on that, as if she'd slammed a door on it in her mind. Now she turned her gaze forward to what was to come.

Over the next two hours, the squadron continued to decelerate at a gentle 1.25 gees. The aliens decelerated at 3.2 gees. The time passed when they would have changed their course or adjusted their plan to fit the new reality Sandy and the cats' atomics had created.

A half hour later, Penny, looking quite chipper and,

munching on her own sandwich, eyed the board with Sandy. "They're holding their course and deceleration," she said.

"I'd have thought they would have adjusted course and gone back to aiming for the next jump," Sandy said.

"Maybe there's nothing out there for them."

"I thought these murderous nuts were all over the galaxy? Scattered few and far between, but all over."

"They are," Penny said, taking a sip of coffee. "But ships belong to wolf packs. It's still an open question as to how well they get along with each other. Even at the Battle of System X, their warships and cruisers formed up by wolf pack."

"You're my chief alien intel honcho," Sandy said. "What do you think they'll do next?"

"I would have thought they'd run. Force us to chase them, maybe lead us into another trap."

"It doesn't look like that's happening."

Penny took a deep breath. "Then I think they'll try a suicide charge."

"A full on Banzai charge, huh?"

"Yep, unless they change course pretty soon for the jump, I think the guy in charge there considered himself and his ships expended from the moment he got the assignment to be bait. That was what he was, orbiting that gas bag in a system we use to slow down in to get into Sasquan. Now that the trap has failed, I doubt if he wants to go home and face the music. Nope, what we're up against is a face-saving charge with no holes barred. To him, he and all the crews with him are already dead. He, and *they*, want to take a few of us with them."

"Even though no one will ever know what he does here."

"I'm just guessing, but I'd say yes. All our research has

failed to identify anything like hope in an afterlife. Faced with oblivion and the fact they haven't had a lot of luck killing us, I expect he'll try to do his damnedest to kill some of us."

Sandy pulled a battle board out of the deck. It showed the space between the gas giant and where BatRon 18 was at present. In a moment, it added the force vectors each of the task forces was generating. Sandy's ships' 1.25 gees deceleration vector was a lot shorter than the 3.2 gee vector on the alien ships.

"Project course twelve hours ahead," Sandy ordered. The aliens were just reaching the gas bag. "Project course for six hours more."

The aliens rounded the gas giant and headed off into space.

"Assume the aliens use a maximum vector toward us."

Even with a vector aimed at Sandy's squadron, the alien could not reach them.

"How much additional braking would they need as they passed the gas giant?" Penny asked as she popped the last of her sandwich into her mouth.

The vector around the huge planet grew longer and the trajectory of the alien ships bent to meet Sandy's ships.

Penny bent close to the board. "Close to four gees it says."

"Could the aliens make four gees?"

Penny shook her head. "At 3.5 gees, their reactors have a tendency to overheat. They can't seem to develop a cooling system to handle more heat."

"What if they deployed some rude form of air brakes and took their dive deeper into the planet's upper-most atmosphere?" Mimzy put in.

"They'd risk burning up the entire ship," Sandy pointed out.

"Admiral, I've seen these folks open their ships to the vacuum of space when faced with defeat. The first ship Kris Longknife ran into was crewed by a multi-generational family. When its attack on us failed, they blew themselves up. The grandfather blew up his entire family of nearly a hundred. When faced with defeat, suicide is their first and last option."

Penny paused to shake her head. "No, ma'am. Sweating out a close pass is nothing. Even if half of the ships overheat and fall apart, it will be enough for them that the other half get a chance to rip our guts out."

"Bastards, huh."

"Paranoid xenophobic bastards with 'Murder or Die,' tattooed on their chests from birth.

"And if we don't let them have a punch at us?" Sandy asked.

"They'll kill themselves."

For the next hour, Penny and Sandy ran through scenarios.

37

After considering all her options, the gas bag turned out to be the deciding factor.

"If we wear away from them," Penny pointed out, "we can avoid combat. They'll likely self-destruct and we can go on our way."

"Go on our way, where?" turned out to be the real question.

If they dodged the alien charge, they'd be headed for the jump. While the nav computer could give them several options with that jump and their speed, there was no data on any of the systems of the stars they might jump to. They would still have a lot of energy on their boats and they'd need to slow down soon and refuel.

"We make too many jumps and there's always a chance we'll run into more aliens. There might be a lot more of them," Penny pointed out.

Sandy grimaced at that thought. "There's always Alwa waiting and the cats that need support. We don't have time to waste playing games with these nut cases."

She thought for a few more moments, then turned back

to her battle board. "Assuming they manage to slow down by diving too damn close to the gas giant, where will we fight them?"

"Likely somewhere between here and there," Penny said waiving vaguely at the battle board. "There are just too many unknowns right now."

Sandy pulled the fuel status of her ships. Most were well past the half-empty mark, "Whatever we do, it's got to include a refueling pass on a gas giant."

"We'll need to slow down for that," Penny said. "And I don't think we want to be going any faster than we have to when we meet those cruisers."

"The faster we go, the fewer chances they have to get shots off at us," Sandy pointed out.

"Yes, ma'am, but the faster they come at us, the fewer shots we get before they can ram us."

"Ram us! You've got to be kidding. Space is way too big for two ships to run into each other in the vastness of space."

"Still, they'll be doing their level best to do it. How much do you want to bet that one of them doesn't get lucky?"

Sandy examined her options. Her squadron had won its battle. Still, her people could die, and would if the aliens were as implacable as her intel officer said they were. Sandy knew the decision she had to make. "We slow the squadron down."

"That's what I would recommend, ma'am."

Sandy sighed. "Comm, send to squadron. We go to 4.1 gees deceleration and set Condition Zed in two minutes."

"Sent."

With serious regrets, Sandy called up her high gee station and did a hurried strip, as did all those around her. She settled into her egg with a fervent prayer that this would be a much shorter stay. On the tick, she gave the order to go to 4.1 gees and felt the oppressive weight force her back deep into the station's cushions. The station might save her from being crushed, but it didn't do anything about the weight of her own flesh on her own body.

Around her, the flag bridge shrunk as the ship concentrated itself down to being the smallest possible killing machine humans had ever created.

As the human squadron decelerated hard, the alien cruisers made a very close pass to the gas giant. They came out glowing bright red on the infrared scanners. Several of them still had some sort of surfaces sprouting out from the hulls. As the ships shot back toward Sandy's ships, the last remaining air brakes fell away.

There were fewer cruisers, however. Sensors counted thirty-one with two out of formation and spinning and what might be three clouds of wreckage headed off in different directions.

For two enemy ships, something had clearly gone wrong. One couldn't seem to hold a steady course, the other's acceleration dropped off and it fell behind. For five minutes or so, the crews of the two ships struggled to correct their problem. Both ships gave up the effort within half a minute of each other. Where they had been were only two expanding super-heated gas clouds.

To Sandy's wide-eyed non-question, Penny answered, "They closed down the magnetic containment field around their reactors and let the plasma eat them. We see a lot of that after a fight with them. As I mentioned before, it's victory or death with these folks."

Sandy could only shake her head slowly. In her head, her heart, her very guts, she struggled to accept the raw facts her eyes presented to her. Someone hated her beyond reason and would risk anything to make her dead.

She'd been in the Navy for a long time, but most of that had been during the long peace. Except for the Battle of Wardhaven, she'd never really had to face the raw fact that death was a part of her job, something she might have to do to others. Something that others might do to her.

It had taken her a while to recover from the shock of the Battle of Wardhaven, but really, she'd gone back to her live and let live beliefs.

Now you better face it, kid. You fight them. You kill them. You win or you and a whole bunch of people the King made your responsibility will die.

Sandy planted that seed, watered it and watched it grow as the hours passed.

With brutal inevitability, the battle hurtled toward Sandy and her command. The alien cruisers reformed themselves into three lines of eight, eight and seven ships each, spaced at five thousand kilometers' intervals. Sandy accepted the challenge and formed her eight ships into a single line with the same interval.

For now, the aliens were decelerating, their sterns aimed away from Sandy's ships. BatRon 18 was likewise decelerating, their sterns pointed toward the alien cruisers.

It was a funny way to charge into battle. They were both blasting away from each other even as their inertia hurtled them toward each other at a closing speed of over 700,000 kilometers an hour.

Sandy did the math and approved of the results. Her squadron's 22-inch lasers would have the alien cruisers in range for a good eighteen minutes. None would survive crossing the killing ground.

The aliens must have spotted that fact about then, too.

The cruisers flipped ship and began accelerating at 3.2 gees toward the humans.

The battle board quickly adjusted to show Sandy's 22-inch lasers would have eleven minutes to cut the aliens to ribbons. Of course, the aliens would have five minutes to use their lasers as the two forces crossed the final expanse of empty space between them.

The alien commander ordered his cruisers up to 3.5 gees.

Sandy considered taking the squadron up to 4.5 gees; none of these aliens would survive to tell any tale. Still, her battlecruisers had been pushing their reactors and cooling pumps hard. The official engineering reports on all the ships showed the power plants functioning well into the yellow. Most were slightly above the mid-range of yellow. The *Yawata* was edging a bit higher.

The aliens might not be able to manage a collision with one of her ships, but a catastrophic engineering casualty could still kill a lot of her people. Sandy nodded to herself and let the two forces stay steady on their present course and acceleration.

She did narrow the killing ground and shave another minute off her firing time.

38

As the alien ships crossed the 200,000 kilometer mark, the maximum range of Sandy's 22-inch lasers, she knew she had five minutes to destroy them before they got close enough to use their own lasers. She had five more minutes before they could try to ram her ships.

That assumed Sandy maintained a steady 4.1 gee deceleration.

"Comm, send to squadron. 'On my mark, go to 4.5 gees deceleration.'" She paused for only a moment to get acknowledgments, then added. "Mark."

In her high gee station, Sandy's body felt every extra ounce that pressed down upon it.

"Comm, send to squadron, 'We will use only aft batteries. For the moment, I do not propose to flip ship and use the forward guns. Advise engineering to make maximum effort to reload the stern chasers.'"

She was limiting herself to only the eight aft lasers of her eight ships: sixty-four. To bring the twelve lasers forward into action she'd have to cut deceleration, flip ship, fire, then flip again and resume deceleration.

Through that entire maneuver, the aliens could be closing on her.

The aft battery should be enough. Sandy estimated she'd get twelve to sixteen salvos from them before the aliens came in range. All that fire from eight battlecruisers should easily destroy thirty-one thin-skinned cruisers.

With luck, they could split their eight-gun salvos between two cruisers

It was such a nice plan.

Then the aliens showed Sandy that they'd learned a thing or two from Kris Longknife.

Just as the cruisers came in extreme range, they started jinksing. They'd zig right, then zag left. They'd rise up or slip down, using their directional rockets to vacate the place they'd been before.

With the first salvo eight human battlecruisers aimed for sixteen alien cruisers. In the second it took the lasers to reach their target, the aliens managed to avoid the space the human fire control computers had calculated they would fill. Sandy's squadron got exactly one alien cruiser. It might have gotten away, too, but it zigged right into the laser beam.

"Somebody has been talking out of school," Penny said. "It looks like the word got out about the way we dodge and weave. Now we've got some of them trying the same trick on us."

"Yeah," Sandy drawled, doing her best to not let the sick feeling growing in her gut impact her commands. "Have Mimzy and Chesty analyze their jitterbugging. How much of a problem can it be if we concentrate eight lasers in the general space around where one cruiser is likely to be?"

"The alien cruisers appear to have a beam of twenty-five

meters," Mimzy reported. "They can accelerate at twenty meters per second per second, which, at face value, gives us a manageable target. However, if they continue their displacing acceleration, it rapidly becomes forty or sixty meters per second. They gain displacement while becoming predictable. They can apply different vectors, up, down, and sideways to complicate our firing solutions."

"Penny," Sandy demanded through clinched teeth, "have your computer feed some sort of firing solution to the guns. We're coming up on reloads. 'Comm to squadron. Concentrate on one ship at a time'."

The reply was so quick, Sandy suspected she was telling skippers to do what they'd already decided to do.

This time, their eight-gun salvos were concentrated on a single bit of space. They bagged two cruisers.

"Can I make a suggestion?" Mimzy ask, ever polite.

"I'm open to anything," was the answer Sandy snapped back.

"I would recommend that I place myself in the targeting sensors and fire control feedback loop. I think I can predict more accurately where the target will be. I could tighten our salvos. Random chance is not working."

"Do it. Have Chesty do the same for the *Essen*."

"Done, Admiral."

Fifteen seconds later, three alien cruisers died.

Twenty-six to go and only three minutes.

Then the aliens got smarter – again.

The next salvo hit only one of the eight cruisers the squadron targeted.

"They have changed their evasion plan," Mimzy reported. "Rather than just using their guidance rockets, they are skewing their ships using the main propulsion. They're honking their nose over one way, and their tails over another, and using their 3.5 gee acceleration to get them out of the target envelope we came up with."

"Expand the spread of the salvoes," Sandy ordered. "We don't need to hose these cruisers down with five or six seconds of solid laser energy. Fire a one-second burst, then nudge the laser right, left, up, and down. Like a machine gun."

"Comm, send to squadron . . ."

"I sent it while you were talking ma'am. You can court martial me later."

"I'll give you a medal."

The squadron fired another salvo from their aft batteries.

Three aliens died.

Again, the battlecruisers waited through the long fifteen seconds as empty capacitors were filled up by the reactors.

They fired again.

No cruisers died!

"They outguessed us again," Mimzy said. "The bastards went to half power. One even cut acceleration entirely. With the ships zigging and zagging now, we missed ahead of all of them."

"Adjust your targeting," Sandy ordered.

She leaned forward in her high gee station.

Maybe I'm becoming too predictable.

"Comm, 'Send to squadron, you fire on my mark'."

"Acknowledged."

"Mimzy, track those bastards," Sandy ordered, while somewhere in the back of her brain she found herself giggling that even a computer had taken to calling the aliens that.

The aliens had resumed their 3.5 gee acceleration as soon as the lasers fell silent. As the fifteen seconds from the last salvo counted down, the aliens switched their zigs to zags and vice versa. At fifteen seconds, they cut their acceleration.

"Course changes identified," Mimzy shouted.

"Fire," Sandy commanded.

Sixty-four lasers stuttered out five one-second bursts.

Five cruisers exploded.

"Take that, you bastards," Mimzy blasted out from Penny's collarbone.

"Penny," Sandy said through a broad grin, "control your computer. I think she's getting overexcited."

"I am not excited," Mimzy said, very primly.

"Study your targets, Mimzy. They're bound to come up with something new."

The aliens did. The next salvo only got one cruiser.

"What happened, Mimzy?" Sandy asked, sourly.

"They cut their acceleration at fifteen seconds, then some of them went back to 3.5 gees. Others cut back some more."

"Again," Sandy muttered to herself, "we are too predictable."

She had used two of her five minutes of free shooting and had only cut the alien force down to nineteen. At this rate, she'd be playing dodge the cruiser with the survivors at way too high a speed.

"They go back to their maximum boost?" Sandy asked.

"Yes, ma'am," Mimzy answered.

"Comm, send to squadron. "Dial the lasers back to half power. Next salvo will be five quick bursts. Then wait two seconds, assess the movement of your target, and fire again."

"Acknowledged," Comm reported immediately.

"Now we see," Sandy whispered softly.

Mimzy seemed to have led her target just right. Still, only one cruiser died in the salvo.

After the lasers fell silent, the aliens went back to their permanent course, 3.5 gee acceleration right at Sandy's squadron.

There was still some jinksing, but nothing like a few seconds ago.

Two seconds later, the squadron lit up eight alien cruisers. Four exploded, two bent in the middle and broke in two and the last two went dead in space. No more jinksing. No acceleration. A few seconds later, they exploded as their skippers switched off the reactors' containment systems.

Ten alien cruisers went to maximum jinksing while they juggled their acceleration from 3.5 gees to as low as .85.

The next two half-salvos missed entirely.

"Squadron, fire by pairs. Gunnery, coordinate between ships."

They got two cruisers that time. Was it a coincidence that the two pairs that had Mimzy and Chesty were the two that scored hits?

With the next double salvo, the computers got their ships again. A third one died under the fire of an unaided pair.

Only five to go.

Of course, the aliens were closing the range to where they could do damage to the reactors and rocket engines on the vulnerable sterns Sandy had pointed directly at their lasers.

Two cruisers died under the next staccato salvo. One to Mimzy, one to one of the other pairs.

Chesty missed. Oh, my.

"Commence Evasion Plan 1," Sandy ordered.

The squadron began its own bouncing up and down,

right and left. Their maneuvering jets were reinforced, as they needed to be, to fight Kris Longknife's way.

Sandy called it right. The three alien cruisers fired their bow guns. Their design being derived by the aliens from the human battlecruisers, they had only fore and aft lasers.

The *Birmingham* took off on a hard-right turn, throwing Sandy against the side of her high gee station so hard that even it couldn't save her from a sharp pain to her shoulder.

The battlecruiser stayed in a hard turn through a full loop, then settled down on a wobbly course that slowly edged around to return to the squadron's main course, but at 3.4 gees.

A few seconds later, the *Birmingham* was back up to 4.1 gees deceleration.

"We took a hit on our port-most pair of engines," Mimzy reported. "They've pulled armor off the hull to reform the plasma conduit and replace the engines. We should be back to 4.5 gee deceleration in a minute."

That would be nice, but Sandy's flagship was now tag end Charlie and likely to be the target for the next shoot, however long it took the aliens to reload.

"Comm, advise the skipper of the *Birmingham* to go to Evasion Plan 3."

"Done, ma'am."

Sandy found her four and a half times normal body weight being pressed to the left, then pushed up as the battlecruiser began its dance. Every time her right shoulder took the turn, pain laced through her body.

Eight battlecruisers against three was stiff odds, but the cruises kept hurtling at them. Sandy split the squadron up. Three ships to target two, the *Birmingham* and *Milan* would target one.

The first half of the salvo went wide as the aliens

dodged, but the second salvo swept two of them. One crumbled, the other exploded. The last cruiser held on, but Mimzy had its number and there was an extra one-second burst that had been pumped into the capacitors even as the lasers pulled the power out.

That last shot nailed the final cruiser.

It sailed on, seemingly unaffected by the hit for a long second.

Then, it disintegrated in a cloud of roiling gas.

For a long moment, the bridge crew around Sandy studied their boards, examining their gauges. They seemed shocked to find no more threats. No murderous aliens screaming at them with deadly intent.

Sandy let a breath out, a long deep sigh, letting the oppressive weight of the 4.5 gees force every cubic millimeter of air from her lungs. Expelling all the tension and fear she'd immersed herself in during the fight.

Empty, she sucked in a breath so sweet with life, she hardly knew what to do with it.

Around her, the bridge crew knew what to do. They let out a cheer.

Sandy didn't join the cheer. She had a command to handle.

"Nav, if you will, what is the best course and deceleration that will slow us enough to make a refueling pass on that gas giant up ahead?"

"One moment, Admiral," and it was a very short moment. "We can go to 2.5 gees with a slight course correction, we'll be down to 100,000 kilometers as we buzz the giant."

"Penny, that's a might bit fast."

"No, ma'am. Kris Longknife did one at that speed. We can do it."

"Here on Alwa Station?"

"You bet, ma'am."

"Then, comm send course and deceleration to the squadron. Advise captains that they may dismiss half their crews to their quarters to clean up. Penny, you hold the fort here for a bit. Then you and Masao can have the next stand down."

Sandy planned to be back on the bridge in half an hour, but Penny had other plans for her boss. She'd heard Sandy cry out in pain when her shoulder was slammed during the *Birmingham's* unscheduled full about turn. Before Sandy had managed to crawl out of the high gee station, a doc from sickbay was at her elbow, looking at the shoulder and doing medical mumbo jumbo. Sandy found herself with help in the shower and a doc taping up her shoulder just as soon as she got dressed.

"Here are pills. You can take them and heal faster, or you can ignore me and feel that shoulder every time you order something faster than three gees for the rest of your life. You are not a kid anymore, Admiral.

"So I'm noticing," Sandy growled. "I've got a watch to relieve. When I can stand down, I'll take your damn pills. Okay?"

"It's your shoulder," the doc said. She promptly packed her bag up and left.

So, it was a little over two hours later before Sandy made it back to the bridge. She settled almost comfortably into her command chair and was very glad to have only two and a half times her weight to manage.

Penny had put the time to good use. Around Sandy things were pretty close to normal. As normal as they ever were on Alwa Station.

39

Three days later, Sandy had weaned herself off her strong painkillers and was using only what any woman used when her period didn't go as pleasant as advertised. Now that she had a clear head, she needed to talk some things out.

She summoned Mondi Ashigara, her operations chief and the skipper of the *Birmingham* to her day quarters, added Penny and Masao to the group and ordered up a pot of soothing tea from the galley.

Her four chosen auditors eyed her curiously as she poured tea and handed each one of them a cup. Mimzy had ordered up a very fancy tea set and Sandy doubted anyone could tell these from a real porcelain tea set.

Last, she served herself.

Once she settled back with her own cup of cooling aromatic delight, she said, "I image all of you are wondering why I called this meeting."

None of them questioned her. Like fine Navy officers, they waited alertly and watched their admiral to see which way the wind was blowing, or, more likely on Alwa Station, what they'd need to blow up next.

"Okay. Let me pose a question. Do any of you have trouble sleeping nights knowing that we have just launched the first nuclear strike in, well, forever?"

Her subordinates looked at each other. It was Penny who first opened her mouth. "I assume that you don't have any qualms about killing a whole lot of aliens that were itching to kill us or using nuclear weapons to change the battle from direct fire weapons to indirect?"

"I'm not losing sleep over any dead aliens. They wanted to murder us. We got to them first. Dead aliens don't count."

"You'll excuse me, Admiral," Sandy said, "but all life counts. The aliens don't give us a chance to count them, but I'm sure that some merciful God somewhere counts every hair on their head."

"My God certainly will not," the *Birmingham's* skipper growled.

"Let us save theology for a long night ashore with a whole lot more and stronger liquids than I can offer," Sandy said. "No, my concern is that I just ordered the first atomic strike since a whole lot of human history got washed under the bridge. Are the cats a bad influence? Is this more of a reason to try to put them back in the bottle until they resolve their history themselves?"

"Resolve their history," Masao added, "by either finding a way for them to put the atomic kami back in the stone or reducing their world to radioactive rubble?"

"I hate those two choices," Sandy's Ops chief added.

Sandy was tired of this meeting going down rabbit holes she didn't care much about. Still, she was the one who ordered up the pot of what was supposed to be relaxing tea.

"Again, folks," she said, "the course of cat history is

something I'll leave to them. They'll either succeed and maybe manage to become yet another species of aliens under our United Society flag or they won't. It's the temptation they dumped in my lap that I would like to muse about with you before I get back to the fleet and we have to do something with our weapons load."

"Admiral Drago suggested we toss them into any sun we passed close to," Penny muttered softly.

"And if we did, there would be no need to develop any policy or doctrine," the ops chief tossed out.

"You can say what you want about those damn missiles," *Birmingham's* skipper said, "but they did just save our bacon. I, for one, would like to have that ace up my sleeve. I like aces up my sleeve."

"Remind me not to play poker with you," bantered back the ops chief.

"I don't cheat at cards. I'm willing to cheat six ways to Sunday when I'm in a fight with those damn murderous bastards," the skipper answered.

"Do we have anything aboard," Penny said, directing the critique back to where Sandy wanted it to go, "or even in our inventory that could have done what the cats' atomics did? It seems to me that direct fire lasers have pretty much dominated the battlefield for several hundred years. We have to be careful using missiles. I think Kris Longknife got some use out of them in the Battle of Wardhaven, but it took a swarm attack to overload their defenses."

"I don't mean to tell the admiral how to suck eggs," the *Birmingham's* captain said, "she having been at Wardhaven for that fight and all, but the after-action reports said the missiles that hit didn't do much damage. A battleship's armor is pretty thick and they just shrugged off the puny warheads the missiles carried."

"I was with Kris Longknife on her fast attack boat," Penny said. "Most of the missiles we scrounged up were obsolete. If we'd had anti-matter armed missiles, we would have toasted those battlewagons a whole lot sooner and lost a lot fewer friends." The young widow's voice broke on the last few words. Silent, she swallowed hard. Masao reached over and squeezed her hand.

Sandy gave her intel chief a few moments to recover. Sandy's destroyer, the *Halsey,* had assisted in the search for life among the wreckage of the fast attack squadron. There hadn't been a whole lot.

Kris Longknife had managed to save about half of her crew. Penny was in that half. Her husband of three days was in the other half.

Sandy continued the conversation after a respectful pause. "Does anyone have any idea how missiles with anti-matter warheads would have fared in our recent battle?" She suspected she knew the answer, but it needed to be on the table.

Her ops chief had a search going on his wrist unit. Sandy had forgotten that though Penny might be out of the meeting for the moment, her computer was not.

"The average detonation value you can expect from an anti-matter warhead is approximately eighteen to twenty-one kilotons. The wide discrepancy is caused by how much the anti-matter particles hit when the containment field is dropped. While it can be solved with more research, no one has felt the need to do it."

Mimzy paused, a practice that she'd learned that let humans catch up with her thoughts that traveled close to the speed of light.

"The thermonuclear bombs the cats gave us were certified to produce twenty megatons, plus or minus a megaton.

We didn't have any real way to evaluate the quality control of the warheads. May I point out that a 20 megaton bomb is approximately a thousand times more destructive than a twenty kiloton anti-matter warhead."

The ops chief whistled. "A thousand times bigger than our biggest."

"Yes," Mimzy said and left it at that.

The ops chief spent a long, quiet minute with his computer. "We only have four hundred anti-matter missiles in our magazines."

"The cats really saved our necks," the *Birmingham's* skipper whispered.

"With atomics, you can pack a very large amount of explosive power into a reasonably small package," Mimzy said.

"Still," Sandy said, "we don't carry a lot of missiles around because lasers tend to wipe them out. We had a rather unique situation. By using 'indirect weapons' and 'carpet bombing', I came across that old word while I was researching atomic usage we were able to dodge under the radar, so to speak, and walk hell and destruction across that crater before they could react."

"If they had mounted a few anti-missile lasers on that ridge . . .," the skipper of the *Birmingham* began, then seemed to run out of words.

"Exactly," Sandy said. "Did we have a unique set of circumstances that, having these atomics on hand, we were able to resolve favorably? Will we be facing circumstances like these very often? Often enough for us to keep these abominations in our magazines?"

Those questions hung in the air.

"We do have the neutron star weapon," Masao said.

"But we've had to be very careful with their use," Penny

said, rejoining the meeting. "When Kris Longknife used three to take down an alien mother ship, we had to damage the thing enough to cut down on its protective fire power. When it was hurting bad, we slipped the three of them in among a wave of fifty or so anti-matter warheads. Even then, one of the neutron bombs got winged and didn't explode as big as the others."

"She has a point," the *Birmingham's* captain said, "Lasers are the king of battle. Missiles need a whole lot of luck or special circumstances to survive in a laser heavy environment."

Sandy took in a deep breath, and let it out as a sigh. "This meeting is going around in circles. You're pretty much saying what I've been thinking. Indirect weapons need a permissive environment to survive on the modern battlefield. Bang for buck, the cats' atomics are the deadliest warheads we could want. The problem is, they come with a huge price. It's much easier to blow away a city than it is to blow away an alien base ship. Is the temptation that some madman will get his hands on them and use them on highly-populated, soft targets too great for us to risk?"

The battlecruiser skipper leaned forward and put his empty tea cup down on the table.

"Like all battlecruisers, the *Birmingham* can carry a load of one or two neutron bombs. I've never carried one, but I've heard one of them turns a fast ship into a pig, and you are no better than a merchant freighter with two of them, and you'd better be careful and slow with what you do. That being said, I'm not one to complain about higher-ups giving us only a few of those big bastards. Now, take that bomb strike we launched. Twenty megatons of un-shirted hell taking off at twenty gees acceleration. Admiral, I know humanity banned those damn things, but we're out here at the end of nowhere fighting a bunch of murderous bastards. If I promise to never take one of those abominations home to human space - not that I'm expecting to go home any time soon - I sure would like to have a dozen or twenty of those puppies tucked away in my magazine to use against these murderous bastards in case of an emergency."

"What's the risk that someone might detonate one aboard?" Sandy asked. "We've got cats. Humans go around the bend. I'm told not every bird likes us. Can you keep them safe?

"If I can get the experts to field strip those things down to their parts, I'd lock all of that up in a magazine that's Smart Metal matrix is controlled by a cipher that would take a month for the best computer aboard to crack," the *Birmingham's* skipper said.

Sandy noticed that Mimzy kept quiet. It was just as well, the captain was saying pretty much what Sandy had concluded herself. Keep them away from human space. Keep them under the tightest controls we humans could develop, but keep them available. The enemy was just too damn adamant about wiping us out as a species. Worse, they were learning from us and growing smarter with each fight.

Sandy would have this discussion again, likely with Admiral Kitano and her fleet bosses. Admiral Benson, too. Maybe that bunch would find a way out that had eluded their boss.

"Thank you, everyone. It's been a most enlightening talk. God willing, we'll figure out a way to walk this sharp edge without getting sliced to pieces."

Her staff dismissed themselves, leaving Sandy staring at the bulkhead.

Things are different on Alwa Station.

Sandy found herself half wishing that this bailiwick still belonged to Kris Longknife, but she couldn't really do it. Kris had been on this hot seat long enough. She deserved time to watch that sweet baby grow into a woman. With any luck that might save her from going down the path that Ray Longknife had stumbled onto.

The Santiagos had paid a high price for the Longknife legend. That didn't mean they believed the damn thing. The Santiagos were probably the only people who saw the underbelly of the Longknife legend, and it wasn't pretty.

This one I'll do myself if all of you damn Longknifes will stay out of my way.

40

A week later, the *Birmingham* lead BatRon 18 through Alpha Jump into the Alwa System.

Sensors slowly built up a picture of normality. No alien reactors in the system. No blood-curdling screams for help. They accelerated for Alwa at 1.25 gees.

Then the message traffic began to come in.

Sandy opened Admiral Kitano's first. She'd left the woman in charge of the Alwa Defense Sector in her absence.

"Boy, am I glad to see you back. Granny Rita is on the rampage and she's got everything in an uproar. We need you down here desperately."

Oh, damn, another Longknife problem!

Mentally, Sandy reached for her Viceroy hat. Whatever the problem was, this was one she'd have to solve without blowing anything up or creating any bodies that needed hiding.

ABOUT THE AUTHOR

Mike Shepherd is the National best-selling author of the Kris Longknife saga. Mike Moscoe is the award-nominated short story writer who has also written several novels, most of which were, until recently, out of print. Though the two have never been seen in the same room at the same time, they are reported to be good friends.

Mike Shepherd grew up Navy. It taught him early about change and the chain of command. He's worked as a bartender and cab driver, personnel advisor and labor negotiator. Now retired from building databases about the endangered critters of the Northwest, he's looking forward to some fun reading and writing.

Mike lives in Vancouver, Washington, with his wife Ellen, and not too far from his daughter and grandkids. He enjoys reading, writing, dreaming, watching grandchildren for story ideas and upgrading his computer – all are never ending.

For more information:
www.mikeshepherd.org
mikeshepherd@krislongknife.com

2017 RELEASES

In 2016, I amicably ended my twenty-year publishing relationship with Ace, part of Penguin Random House.

In 2017, I began publishing through my own independent press, KL & MM Books.

I am delighted to say that you fans have responded wonderfully. We have sold over 20,000 copies of the five e-novels. In 2018, I intend to keep the novels coming,

We started the year with **Kris Longknife's Replacement** that tells the story of Grand Admiral Sandy Santiago as she does her best as a mere mortal to fill the shoes left behind on Alwa Station by Kris Longknife. Sandy has problems galore: birds, cats, and vicious alien raiders. Oh, and she's got Rita Nuu-Longknife as well!

February had a novelette. **Kris Longknife: Among the Kicking Birds** was part of Kris Longknife: Unrelenting. However, it went long and these four chapters were cut to one short paragraph. I hope you enjoy the full story.

Rita Longknife: Enemy Unknown was available in March and is the first book of the long-awaited Iteeche War series. Rita has had enough of Ray Longknife gallivanting around the universe. No sooner is little Al born, than ships start disappearing. Is it pirates or something more sinister? Rita gets herself command of a heavy cruiser, some nannies, and heads out to see what there is to see.

April had another short offering, **Kris Longknife's Bad Day**. You just knew when Kris asked for a desk job that she'd have days like you have at the office. Well, here's one that will bring you up to date on the technical developments in the Royal US Navy, as well as silly bureaucratic goings on. In the first draft of **Emissary**, these were the opening chapters, but I found a better opening and this got cut. Enjoy!

Kris Longknife: Emissary began an entirely new story arc for Kris and was available May 1. Here is the story of what it takes to get Kris out from behind a desk. And for those of you betting in the pool, you'll get your answer. More I cannot say.

June brought you Abby Nightingale's view of things around Alwa in **Kris Longknife's Maid Goes on Strike.** You knew sooner or later this was going to happen.

July had another book set in Alwa. As **Kris Longknife's Relief,** Sandy Santiago, continues to battle aliens of various persuasions and not a few humans.

Rita Longknife: Enemy in Sight was released in September and sought to resolve the unknowns left by Enemy Unknown as humanity slipped backwards into a war it does not want and may not be able to win.

Kris Longknife's Maid Goes on Strike and Other Short Stories, is a collection of four short stories: Maid Goes on Strike, Ruthie Longknife's First Christmas, Among the Kicking Birds, and Bad Day. These were available in October all under one ebook cover for a great price.

Kris Longknife: Admiral was available in November. In this adventure, Kris is up to her ears in warships, enemies, and friendlies who may be not as friendly as she'd like, as battlecruisers square off against battlecruisers. A fight where both sides are equal is a bloody fight that often no one wins.

Work is already going on for a January 18 release of Kris Longknife's Successor. March will have the next book in the Iteeche War, and May will continue Kris's adventures in the Iteeche Empire with Kris Longknife: Warrior.

Stay in touch to follow developments by following Kris Longknife on Facebook or checking in at my website www.mikeshepherd.org.

I hope to soon have a mailing list you can sign up for.

Printed in Great Britain
by Amazon